NASH - Grass and supergrass

D1827652

GRASS AND SUPERGRASS

Peeper has never been in the big league and most likely never will be. He chooses his tickles with care, keeps out of the headlines and manages to put together a living in a town where there are enough active rogues to keep him going for ever.

But all that changes when a Supergrass comes on the scene and starts to put the finger on every crook in town. Detective Sergeant Boggis is too busy to bother with Peeper. Pretty soon there's nobody left to keep tabs on – and redundancy stares Peeper in the face.

Until things start to go wrong as they always do, even for a supergrass – and that's when Peeper is there to hold the bits together and make whatever profit he can in the process.

Once again, Padder Nash takes a series of events so tangled as to seem beyond sorting – and brings them to order. He also distils a deal of humour out of a basically hazardous situation.

Grass and Supergrass

PADDER NASH

ROBERT HALE · LONDON

0 709 013 922

© Padder Nash 1984
First published in Great Britain 1984

ISBN 0 7090 1392 2

Robert Hale Limited
Clerkenwell House
Clerkenwell Green
London EC1R 0HT

Photoset in North Wales by
Derek Doyle & Associates, Mold, Clwyd
Printed in Great Britain by
Photobooks (Bristol) Ltd, Barton Manor, St Philips, Bristol
and bound by WBC Bookbinders Ltd

ONE

Crime fascinates me.

Nothing to boast about? No, I suppose it fascinates a lot of other people too, but for me it has a very special attraction because I make my living from it. Hold it, now. Don't switch off on the grounds that you're honest Joes and don't want anything to do with criminals. I don't *commit* crime. (I used to, but I don't any more – not if I can help it.) But it's still my bread and butter.

There's a lot of it about (crime, I mean) and I hear about fresh outbreaks all the time. That's because I listen hard. By keeping my ear to the ground the way I do, I manage to get hold of the gen on all aspects of it; current trends, attractive items, market values, disposal channels, people who do it and people who suffer from it, that sort of thing. But for all my deep interest in the subject I don't often see crimes happen – which makes the raid on Hymie Crewe's gambling palace and moneychanging emporium an event of rather special importance.

I'd only gone there to oblige Stella.

Now I'm not too big on horses myself. Oh, they're fine animals and they make a handsome spectacle when they go thundering in droves round Ascot or Aintree, but they never seem to raise in me that odd mixture of hope and agony the regular punter suffers from. Stella doesn't gamble much, either, but she is a creature of whims and sudden inspirations, and when she noticed that a horse called Stellar was running in the three-thirty at Newmarket she convinced herself it must be an omen. (Stella – Stellar, you see. Or maybe you don't see, and who am I to blame you.) Anyway, Stella got this bee in her bonnet – and since she wouldn't be seen dead in a betting shop she switched her charm on me, which is why I toddled round to Hymie Crewe's place to put her a few bob on Stellar's nose.

I was there long before the race so I hung about for a while to see if the odds would improve. If the chance arose, I meant to go out of there with more money in my pocket than I brought in. Not for a minute did I suppose I was alone in that aim, but some people, it seemed, weren't even prepared to leave it to chance.

The door burst open and three customers came in, in a bunch. They had woolly masks over their faces – just like the old Balaclava helmet but with narrow eye slits – and two of them were carrying double-barrelled twelve-bore shotguns, to which they'd carried out structural improvements by lopping off most of the butt and half the barrel. The third bloke didn't have such a fancy tool. All he had was an automatic pistol – a Luger at a guess, but don't take my word for it – and he waved it around like he was spraying flies. Believe me, when that sort of customer comes in, everybody notices them. I pretended not to – by stooping and shoving my face in a sporting paper – but I could see everybody else had swung round to have a look, so I did the same.

"This is a stick-up," the bloke with the Luger shouted, a bit unnecessarily. "Back against the wall, all of you."

Nobody moved – like me they were back against the wall to start with – but I have to admit my wool-covered friend had stamped his authority on the gathering. People were beginning to feel nervous. I was aware of at least three trembling knees – two of them my own – and nobody was bothering to smile.

"Anybody makes a move, I blast 'em," the man said, whereupon he advanced to the counter and his two henchmen moved to cover the rest of the room. "A couple of those big bags," he said, nodding to the nearest cashier, "and stuff the money in."

"All of it?" It was a silly question, but the poor bloke was scared witless and babbling. The stick-up merchant made a sound through his wool cover that I took to be a sneer.

"All of it. Not the brown stuff, but everything else."

✻   ✻   ✻

You must have wondered what special thoughts pass through people's minds when they're standing there doing nothing at the point of a gun. I can't speak for others, only for myself, and I have an idea that my thoughts that day in Hymie Crewe's place were very much non-standard. Oh, I had all the usual ones, such as, *pray heaven they don't start shooting* and *where's the nearest laundry if they do?* But behind all that I was having a whole battery of other thoughts which were a deal more palatable in nature.

What a hell of a chance to turn a few quid, was my primary thought, closely followed by, *won't Bert Boggis be chuffed*.

I'd better explain that Detective Sergeant Albert Boggis is a business associate of mine. We've been in partnership for a lot of years and if we can keep it going for a lot more years maybe we'll finish up friends one day. So far, our relationship's a bit uneasy. Him being a cop – and ugly with it – Bert Boggis isn't the sort of bloke I'd want to be seen around with – and me being a bit of a lag with some nasty black entries in the C.R.O. files, I'm not Bert's idea of the perfect boozing mate. All the things we have in common could be rolled up in a fag paper and disposed of in three puffs. To be honest, the only reason we're able to work together at all is because I have things Bert wants – and vice versa. Well, I don't so much have information as the ability to scratch around and find it – and Bert doesn't so much have money as the know-how to screw it out of his bosses, or insurance companies, or what have you, but between us we manage to show a profit over the years.

And here was a live show of very high grade information. It was better than just an armed robbery happening before my very eyes, it was the latest in a long string of such robberies. For weeks, Boggis had been leaping on my back with sad tales about how somebody was ripping the town apart and getting away with so much money that we'd soon be reduced to bartering in order to live. And I'd done my best to help him with it, because I don't like loot going astray any more than Boggis does, but all my best efforts had been in vain, as they say. Nobody was chattering. No out-of-work layabouts were buying new cars. None of our local crime tycoons were recruiting helpers and no strange, ugly or depraved faces had made their appearance in the pubs, clubs or hush-places I frequented.

Half the trouble was the commodity involved. It's a well known fact that for freshly nicked fags or spirits you might get half price if you're lucky, but for a fiver you can get five ones anywhere – and for a one, a hundred pence. But it goes far deeper than that. Money – and especially the well used sort that tends to come out of betting shops – is very easy to get rid of. There are no middlemen to mess around with, no labels to alter, no storage space to be found (other than your own sky-rockets, that is) and nothing incriminating to be seen even if you're searched. Therefore, all the negotiations that normally give rise to leaks through the grapevine are eliminated if you stick to money. That was why the recent spate of robberies had got away from me. Money was bad news. And don't try telling me that no news is good news.

But all of a sudden my luck seemed to have changed. Here was I with a grand-stand seat at the latest match. All I had to do was take a close look at the three cowboys involved, see something I could recognise and then keep the detail in my mind.

Let me admit, it wasn't easy. The two henchmen – the ones with the sawn-off shot-guns – must have patronised the same tailor, or been present when a load of jeans and leather jackets fell off the back of a lorry, and even their shoes were identical pairs of brown brothel-creepers. I saw faint hope in the backside of one of them (and before you get the wrong idea, let me say I wouldn't give tuppence a truck-load for male backsides) because it had a certain shape about it that reminded me of – Hell, no. He was doing a three-year stretch wasn't he? But you can never be sure these days. The second was on the short side, which could have meant he was either … or … and might also have meant that he was a complete stranger. The boss man – the bloke with the Luger – was six feet tall, give or take a thou, and it occurred to me how sad it was that so many of our local thugs are around that height. He was wearing overalls – new overalls to judge from their condition – and black leather shoes with a nice sheen on them.

So I wasn't doing awfully well as a witness – and about that time it occurred to me that I was making my interest in them a bit too obvious, because the nearest bloke came over real close and began to glare at me. It's a funny feeling being glared at by something that looks like an outsize coconut, a bit frightening too. I could see his eyes, but if they held any sort of message for me it was no more than, *Keep your nose out, Buster*. So I offered him a weak grin and a shrug of the shoulders and he moved away. Things were not panning out well for future business with Bert Boggis. When I saw him later and told him how much I knew he'd be hard pressed to be pleased. Surely to God I ought to be able to spot something. I took a surreptitious look at the men's hands – six hands in all and all on view – but there was not a ring or a wart, a wound, a tattoo or a twisted knuckle. And then I got lucky.

There came the sudden crack of a pistol shot.

My knees sagged and I slid down the wall, my eyes busy on my shirt front for the first sight of gushing blood. There wasn't any, and I looked up in time to see what had happened. A grey-haired old chap standing a few yards away from me had done something so risky that it made my guts churn to think of it. He'd grabbed at the mask of the nearest bloke and ripped it off. Meantime, boss man who had seen this happening took his eyes off the cashier long enough to loose a shot at the grey-haired bloke. He'd hit him in the arm and the poor old sod was standing there with blood spreading over his jacket sleeve and dripping off his fingers.

That incident signalled the end of the affair. In a

mood of 'coming – ready or not' the boss grabbed two bags of cash from the counter, turned and ran out. The other two went with him, the second still struggling to get his mask back on. As the door closed behind them the scene came to life. People rushed towards the old man and started doing things with his arm; sympathy and praise was heavy on every lip; a galvanised cashier touched a late button and the alarm bell began to sound its useless warning.

I sneaked out and went my thoughtful way. So many problems had begun to occur to me that my head was in a turmoil. There might be something in it for me, but not before I'd spent a lot of time going over the snags and ironing them out. I needed time to think, room to think and something to drink to lubricate the wheels. There was always Vince Skinner's place. I set off to go there.

And Stellar? Well, he romped home at twenty-to-one – and I'd clean forgotten to put the bet on.

TWO

Over the years I've spent a great deal too much time –
not to mention too much money – in Skinner's caff.
I've also assaulted my stomach and paved the way for
ulcer's in later life.

The Golden Roof Restaurant, to give it the name it
was born with, is an ill-patronized dump of a place that
occupies a corner site in that part of town which used
to be the slums and is now a vast rag-bag of old
houses, new factories, building sites and clear patches
still being offered for redevelopment. For some
purposes the place might have been ideal – sewage
disposal, rag-sorting and maggot-breeding spring
readily to mind – but as a place to eat and drink it is a
bit on the manky side and probably never has been up
to much, even in the early days when it had a gold
painted ceiling, a readable name board over the
entrance, decent furniture and a more reputable
proprietor.

But I can't go back that far. In that dismal building,
shaped like a row of hen cabins without intermediate
walls, Vince Skinner has wobbled around and sold his
slops for more years than I can count. The ceiling still
has traces of gold paint – you can find them if you look
hard among the cobwebs, chewing-gum darts and
fragments of flung food and drink – but nothing else
remains of the place's former glory – if it ever had any.

Vince is a fat man. To be brutally frank, the word *fat* doesn't go anything like far enough to describe him. *Obese* falls short too, and *mountainous* implies a beauty that Vince hasn't got. I'm tempted to use *elephantine*, but that doesn't quite fit either, because he's shorter and fatter than that – and anyway, I don't like insulting elephants. If I explain that he can't fall over without rolling in a complete circle and landing back on his feet you'll perhaps get the idea. His vastness is said to have come about by over consumption of his own sandwiches, pies and sausage rolls which, if true, must at least credit him with more courage than the average man. I know he drinks his own beverage because I've seen him at it – and if you think I should have said *beverages* you're mistaken. There really is only one, and he tarts it up in some mysterious way to pass as tea or coffee according to the customers' wishes.

Why do I go there at all? You may well ask. There's no simple answer, so I'll give you a complicated one. To begin with, Vince's dump attracts so little custom that it has never been known to be full, even in the height of the tourist season. I once saw about twenty people in there – the Coronation, I think it was – and the sight was so unusual that people still talk about it. You can always find an empty table in a quiet corner at Skinner's caff, and that alone is sometimes worth a lot. But mainly I go because of the class of person I meet. The Golden Roof Restaurant is a prostitutes' parlour, a thieves' kitchen, a layabouts' lair and a gossips' gallery. The grapevine has a permanent receiver terminal there – and for all practical purposes it's a 'no-go' area for the cops. I'd better add that the police are not *afraid* to go there – they're too genteel and well brought up to *want* to go.

I don't say much when I go to Vince's place. My

mouth may open pretty often and words may issue in quite a stream, but they are only words of greeting, platitudes, observations on matters of no importance. It's what other people say that matters to me, as well as what they do. The things I see and the things I hear are often very useful to me in my trade. In fact, if they ever decide to close the place down I shall more than likely have to go out of business.

On the day of the robbery I went to Skinner's caff for the secondary reason – that I required peace, quiet and wet lips. I gave Vince a cheery 'hello' (it pays to keep in with the fat slob) bought a cup of gunge, retired to a corner table and started to ponder the problems that faced me.

I knew damned well who had carried out the robbery at Hymie Crewe's betting shop. Well, it would have been pity help me if I'd seen Alistair Proud's face – which I had, very clearly – and failed to identify him. But as things stood, I couldn't do anything about it. The snag was that Proud – Swanky Alice as he was more often known – knew that I knew that he ...

Long before his unmasking, Swanky Alice had glared at me through the stitches of his face cover and although I hadn't known it was him, he'd been very well aware that I was me. It must have tickled him, at that time, to think that he was carrying out a big job with me looking on – and that I was totally ignorant of the fact. What a change his spirits must have undergone, a few minutes later, when that brave old sod who ought to have known better had whipped his mask off without as much as *by your leave*.

But in laying Alistair Proud's face bare before the world and settling all my doubts about identity, the old chap had also dropped a big stumbling block in my path. I daren't go to Bert Boggis at any price. If I did,

Boggis would find Proud and feel his collar, in which case Proud would say to himself, *I wonder who shopped me*, in which case it would take him about three tenths of a second to come up with the right answer, in which case I could wave good-bye to a happy life. It seemed a criminal waste that I should have such hot intelligence in my possession and not be able to use it. If I didn't use it – if I didn't seek out Bert Boggis and put the squeak in – I'd be missing the chance of a very nice rake-off. So it was a straight choice – money against happiness. I was too sad to go one way and too greedy to go the other.

*   *   *

Time passed. A great deal of time.

I fell to thinking about the second and third members of the masked gang who had robbed Hymie Crewe's betting shop. Having identifed Alistair Proud, it stood to reason that I would have known the others if I'd had the chance to see their faces. But I really ought to know them anyway. I had a fair idea which crowd Swanky Alice ran around with – and although they numbered a hell of a lot more than two, I had the evidence of my own eyes to help me differentiate. The boss – the chap with the Luger – was hard to pinpoint, since I had nothing on him but his height and build. I could think of three or four among Swanky Alice's circle of acquaintances who might have fitted in that mould, so it was a case of remembering each one in turn and doing a mental comparison. After a while I gave that up, because I thought it might be easier trying to put a name to the third member of the gang. In his case there weren't so many alternatives. He was the one with the oddly shaped rear end that I'd remarked about before – and damn me if I didn't still think it was one bloke – and one bloke only.

In this way I'd mulled over the names and pedigree of half the local criminal fraternity and I was part-way through my third mug of Skinner's dreadful brew when the situation changed. I'd told myself for the hundredth time that the bloke with the odd bottom had got to be Bent Nelson – when I saw a figure pass by Skinner's front window and turn in at the door. Even as he stood in the doorway I recognised him. He was Bent Nelson.

Nelson didn't look in my direction. He strode across to the counter and thumped hard for service – and I was so busy gawping at Nelson and remarking on the amazing coincidence that had brought him here that I failed to notice the two others who had followed him in. The first thing I knew about them, was when I picked up that odd, tingly feeling that somebody was watching me – and when I looked up they were right there, standing by my table.

"Wotcha, Peeper," Swanky Alice said, grinning at me.

"Hi, Alice."

And right there, in that little exchange, lies a first class example of how curious human foibles can be. I hate to be called 'Peeper' because the name has certain unpleasant, even perverted sexual connotations. Bert Boggis invented the name, many years ago – and for reasons completely different from those I've just referred to, I do assure you – since when the blasted thing has waxed and multiplied until nobody ever calls me by anything else. Although I hate the name, I've had to live with it. These days I never bridle or complain – except to Boggis – but I still cringe inwardly when I hear it, and I suppose I always shall.

But if I were a big, tough hombre – which Alistair Proud is, and I'm not – I'd hate to be called *Alice*. Alice is a tart's name after all, and blokes like Proud might be expected to go off at the deep end when saddled with a tart's name. But Swanky Alice didn't give a damn – had never given a damn as far as I ever heard – and he'd have considered you less than matey if you *didn't* call him Alice. Never make the mistake, though, of including the first bit. The 'Swanky' tag is useful as a means of identification when you're talking *about* him to some third person, but never, never use it to his face. If I'd been daft enough to respond, 'Hi, *Swanky* Alice,' he'd more than likely have knocked me off my chair.

All of which is a good way of introducing the third member of the recently arrived trio. Unlike Proud, or Bent Nelson who was still at the counter, chatting with Vince Skinner, (Bent, by the way, wasn't intended to describe his nature but is short for *Bentley*) the third chap had a very ordinary name. John Field.

Such an ordinary name, in fact, that I'd more than once wondered how the hell he'd managed to get away with it. There were enough possible puns on 'Field' surely, and even on 'John', for an inventive mind to come up with an apt soubriquet – but in Field's case it had never happened. And the strange thing was that all the familiarity that normally swells from a nickname, had swollen – in his case – from his real name. *John Field* had somehow become a very distinctive name indeed. Everybody knew John Field.

Field had got rid of his overalls but he was still wearing the shiny black shoes and I didn't have to be a Sherlock Holmes to describe with great accuracy what he'd been doing in Hymie Crewe's place a few hours earlier. The Luger was missing too, I was very pleased to see. There was no bulge under his arm or at his waistline. Swanky Alice and Bent Nelson had ditched their sawn-off shotguns as well, but they were both still wearing the jeans and leather coats they'd worn to pull the job. Some people have a hell of a lot of cheek – and they're the people who always get away with it.

All these thoughts had passed through my mind in the twinkling of an eye that elapsed before Swanky Alice spoke again, and as a result I was forewarned – didn't leap and whinny at his next question.

"Backed any good winners lately, Peeper?"

"I don't bother much with the gees," I said.

"But you get in Crewe's place off and on, don't you?"

"Oh sure – off and on. When I can afford to lose a bob or two."

"You lose anything this afternoon?"

"No. Not so you'd notice."

"But you did call in there, earlier on, didn't you, Peeper?"

"That's right. Fancied a flutter. I do, sometimes."

"Anything happen while you were in there? Any trouble, I mean? You'd surely have seen it if there was."

Proud seemed to ask that all-important question three times in three different ways. It was as though he was challenging me to give the answer he wanted and at the same time allowing me enough thinking time to be sure I got it right. I didn't require any thinking time. I knew damned well what Proud was after – and in return for an undamaged skin I was happy to give it to him. Even so, the air was electric. Proud and John Field could hardly wait for what I was going to say. Bent Nelson, who was too far away to hear the conversation but must have sensed that a crucial point had been reached, took half a dozen paces in my direction and even fat old Vince Skinner fixed me with his piggy eyes.

"Nothing happened as far as I'm aware," I said.

"That's a good thing – a bloody good thing," Swanky Alice breathed. "You should remember that, Peeper, for your own good."

I'd been prepared to sell myself cheaply. As a man of honour I'd have said anything to keep the occasion amicable, and it was enough for me that they were satisfied with the answers. It came as a complete surprise, therefore, when John Field reached into an inside pocket, came out with a bundle of tatty notes and dropped them on the table in front of me.

"Thanks for the loan, Peeper," he said. "You'll find it's all there – with interest. No, you don't have to sign a receipt."

I hadn't moved, so his remark about receipts was superfluous. I hadn't even touched the wad of notes. I just sat there, looking at it, and while I was so engaged the three of them went out. I picked it up then. Well, what the hell can you do when somebody drops wages in your lap? I didn't bother to count it at that stage, I just stuffed it in my pocket, waved at Vince Skinner and walked out of the caff.

*   *   *

One hundred and one pounds. I counted it three times to make sure, but it came out the same each time. They'd meant to give me a straight hundred, that was obvious, and somebody had miscounted, but I had no intention of giving them the odd quid back.

I fought quite a battle with myself about whether I ought to give the whole wad back. I'd like you to know that this was not so much a battle of conscience as a problem of expediency. I'm no plaster angel – never have been – and I don't turn away loot simply because it wasn't honestly obtained. But I do suffer from a yellow streak, and if there's an element of risk attached to any deal I always weigh it carefully before I go firm. In the present case I was handling hot property, no doubt about that. What I had in my hands was part proceeds of a very recent armed robbery, and if it were ever proved that I'd taken the money I could depend on free board and lodgings for a long time. To a very large extent I had Boggis to blame for my troubled state of mind. He was the one who, over the years, had preached contractual honesty to me. *Never get your own fingers dirty, Peeper*, he'd always insisted. *Find out and report, but never get involved yourself. We've got a good arrangement going here, but if you ever take an active part in crime you'll blow the roof off it. So don't come running to me when things go wrong. You'll have yourself to blame and I won't lift a finger to help you.*

He meant it, too – as much as Bert Boggis ever means anything. I hadn't always been able to follow his advice to the letter – and more than once he'd pulled strings to get me out of a tight spot – but I knew damned well that if ever the crunch came – the time when he had to choose between me and his own neck – he'd throw me to the wolves.

But apart from the gypsy's warning I'd had from Bert, there was another very important aspect. By taking the money, I'd compromised myself with John Field and his unsavoury mates. For ever, after this, they'd be able to point a finger at me and call me one of their own. I *was* one of their own. They'd bought me.

In the end, I decided to keep the money. Why? Well, because a hundred quid is a hundred quid in anybody's language and I didn't see why I should deprive myself. After all, I couldn't shop this mob – for very different reasons – so what did it matter that I took money to keep my mouth shut? Besides, they were old and very dirty notes, and they'd obviously passed through thousands of hands before they reached mine. It would be a crime not to keep that money circulating. I had a positive patriotic duty to take it, spend it and thus do my own little bit to help a troubled economy.

A little later, it was driven home to me what an excellent decision I'd made. My feet had been leading me away from Stella's place and the chances are I'd never have gone there if I hadn't seen her name in a paper that a bloke at a bus stop was holding. It wasn't Stella, of course, but Stellar – and by peeking over this bloke's shoulder I learned that the horse had won – and at what odds.

Twenty to one – One hundred quid against a fiver.

Well, the Lord giveth and the Lord taketh away. I took out the spare quid, then marched straight off to the Albion and gave the rest of the wad to Stella. I smiled broadly, sharing the thrill of her luck. And anyway, I'd made a quid for myself, hadn't I?

"Is it all here, James?" she said in that half-stern, half-puzzled way that Stella has. "I thought it was customary to return the stake as well."

"Sorry, Stella."

I fished in my pocket and passed over another fiver.

THREE

James is not my real name, and nobody ever calls me that but Stella. Many moons ago, when I was younger and fitter – and Stella was younger and fitter too – I had the need to call myself something. Stella had just introduced me, for the first time, to the delights of her boudoir and to the appetizing fry-up in the kitchen that always follows a trip upstairs. I'd only just met the woman and I hadn't made my mind up whether I wanted to go on meeting her or not, so when she asked me my name I gave her the first lie that came into my head – and she's been calling me *James* ever since.

When our little tie-up first started it was casual. Stella was a fancy bit on the side and I was somebody she fancied having a fling with. We might have tired of each other inside a week or two, in which case we'd have parted as friends. But it didn't happen that way. We tagged along together in a very satisfactory fashion, neither trying to trap the other, until we made the discovery that we were each part of the same natural twosome – and since then we've stayed that way. It's a comfortable, amicable arrangement from my point of view and I don't see how it could be bettered. Stella would be a wee bit happier if I married her – and I have to admit I keep kidding her along that it might happen some day – but there's no way I can marry Stella. There's Doreen, you see.

But let me stay with Stella. I'll tell you about Doreen later. Stella keeps a flea-pit of a doss-house on the edge of town. She wouldn't like to hear me calling it a doss-house. She thinks the Albion Hotel is a very salubrious residential establishment, but in that respect her opinions – like her eyesight – are a bit dim. If I stretch a point, the bricks and mortar part of the Albion lacks nothing but pointing, painting and a bit of touch up repair, but the true nature of an hotel is measured in terms of its clientele – and that's where the Albion scores heavily – as a flea-pit of a doss-house. The men who stay there (I have known the occasional woman lodger, but usually it's men) are the fly-by-nights, the down-and-outs, the ne-er-do-wells and all the rags, tags and bobtails of a degenerate society. That's the reason why they're there – because they are the fly-by-nights, etc. Stella is a reformer at heart, and nothing pleases her more than to take a man when he's down and try to mould him into a pillar of society. Her success rate is not of the highest. Not to be too unkind, if she managed to mould one more pillar she'd only need four others to make five.

But the readiness is all, as somebody with a beard and a busy pen once said, and if ever you want to clap eyes on a happy woman, go and watch Stella as she ministers to her flock. Never a thief but she'll talk him into looking for honest work, never a fire-raiser but she'll teach him an aversion to flames, never a flasher but she'll persuade him to fuse-weld the zip on his flies. And they listen to her – my God, how they listen – but the minute her back's turned, back they go to their wicked ways.

Which, in a manner of speaking, is where I come in. As I mentioned earlier, I take an especial interest in crime, and where better to indulge that interest than in a place like the Albion Hotel where – if you hang about long enough – every rogue in town will eventually pass by? I've tangled with more than my share of rogues at the Albion, and the fact that I regularly tangle with Stella too, makes it all so easy. All I need to do is give Love to Stella and keep her in the dark about Commerce. The latter is extremely important. If she ever found out how much information I pick up at the Albion – and what I do with it – she'd start to mould me as well – and I'd finish up the size and consistency of a piece of camel shit.

So I stayed at the Albion long enough to let Stella show her gratitude for the money I'd won her, then I left and spent an hour or two on the town. It would have been on the cards for me to keep an assignment with Bert Boggis – I was overdue in fact, and I had a quid or two to come for a little job I'd put his way a few days earlier – but I kept away, because somehow I couldn't face Boggis. It would have been different if I'd had something useful to pass on – such as the names of the armed gang currently troubling him – but I didn't have any information to pass on, and I was suffering pangs of conscience over it.

The pubs were well into the evening session when I crawled out of one of them and went for a stroll through the fish market. The fish market is no such thing, by the way. There used to be fish-stalls there, back when Adam was a lad, but these days it's just a rather busy part of town centre, where young tearaways do much of their motor-biking and their wenching, where drunks foregather to celebrate their drunkenness, where a number of the local girls ply their trade and where the bobbies walk about in twos. I was right at the heart of the throng, within sight of a great many evil faces, when I was surprised to see an old battered Ford Consul draw up alongside me. I felt no need to check the registration number. Only one person ever drove a heap of crap like that, and there the bugger was, grinning at me through the window.

"You're Peeper, aren't you?" he said pleasantly.

You inconsiderate bastard, Bert Boggis. Not only do you saddle me with that blasted name; you also call me by it in front of half the criminal fraternity of the entire county. And what the hell do you mean by singling me out in this obvious, public way?

"That's what ignorant people sometimes call me," I said, grudgingly.

"I thought it was you. Jump in the back."

Jump in the lake, you narrow-gutted sod, I said, but I didn't say it out loud. Even mortal insults can smack of familiarity, and showing familiarity toward a cop is asking for trouble, especially in a crowded fish market. Not being entirely without marbles I smothered my finer feelings and said:

"What for? What's it about?"

"I want words with you, that's all. I need your help."

"Come off it, officer. How can I help you?"

That *officer*, was a carefully calculated try-on. Boggis was wearing his usual plain clothes – if the most dreadfully matched and ill-fitting clobber can be called 'plain' – and the question might possibly arise, *how had I known he was a copper?* But I knew that question would *not* arise – not in present company, anyway. Boggis was a familiar face to the surrounding hooks and rogues, his tatty old banger even more familiar, and since most knowing people would number me with the ungodly, I was *entitled* to recognise Detective Sergeant Boggis. I wasn't entitled to be chummy with him, that's all.

"You're a witness," he said, cheeky as hell. "There was an armed robbery today – at Crewe's betting shop – and you saw it."

"Who says I did?"

"I say you did. Now look here, Peeper. I've been nice to you so far, but that was on the assumption that you'd co-operate. If you won't play, I've got ways and means. So what's it to be? Are you coming – or do I have to fetch you?"

I'd done enough to convince the populace that it was a straight lift, with no connivance on my side, and that I was going with Boggis against my will, so now I climbed into the back seat of the Consul and Boggis drove away. He was alone in the car, but we travelled in silence. With all those people watching me I didn't want to be seen in earnest conversation, and later, when the streets were quieter I was so flaming mad at him I couldn't trust myself to speak. I just sat there, glaring at the back of his scrawny neck and wishing I had a cheese wire to garotte the stupid sod with. At the nick, in the public part, I played the bewildered witness – and it wasn't too difficult, because I *was* bloody bewildered. Boggis took me through to an interview room and closed the door. Then I exploded.

"You brainless dick. Who but a cretin would pull a crackpot bloody trick like that? I've known you pull some dangerous strokes, Bert Boggis, but this was king of 'em all. What the hell possessed you to grab me in the street, you half-witted bloody toad?"

I merely present a sample – an excerpt to convey the general idea. While I rated him, Boggis sat and looked at me impassively. Laughter was as near his lips as it ever gets. He never allows amusement to broaden his face – for fear of cracking his death mask I suppose – but the lips tremble, the cheeks twitch, the eyes become noticeably less dull. It's a strange thing, but I don't think we've ever been mutual about mirth. If he twitches I tend to become angry. If I laugh at him he takes the huff – and it might last for days.

"… and it's no laughing matter, Boggis," I finished.

"You're right, Peeper. It isn't. If this sort of thing happened in wartime, on active service, they'd put you up against the nearest wall and fill you with holes."

"What the hell are you drivelling about?"

"I'm talking about treason. That's what you committed today, you treacherous little sod. I've just about had a bellyful of you, Peeper. I pay you good money – I'm entitled to a bit of loyalty."

"You pay me peanuts," I snapped. (It wasn't entirely true, but I've never been averse to attacking the bastard with lies.) "I've stuck my neck out for you a million times – taken risks you wouldn't ask a stunt-man to take – and all for a few measly quid and a promise of discretion. So what happened to the promise, Bert? Where's all this confidentiality you always boasted about? You've tired of working with me, haven't you? You're trying to get me rubbed out."

"I brought you in on purpose, dim-wit. I had to do it, for the very good reason that you should have come to me – and you didn't."

"And why in God's name should I have come to you?" I looked hard at Boggis. I knew the answer to my question, even before I asked it, but I wasn't going to let him think I'd conceded the point.

"It was your duty, Peeper," he said, wearing his earnest face for effect. "You had the dope on the Crewe job – and the minute you got it, you owed it to me. That's the deal we've got running."

"You've been misinformed, Bert. I know nowt about that job."

"Yes you do. You were there. You saw it all."

"Who says so?"

"I say so, for Christ's sake – and not without good supporting evidence. Two of the clerks know you by sight. They described you. If you must know, they fed you to me as a suspect. You were in there for quite a while, it seems, and you never had a bet. That made them suspicious. They suggested you were probably a look-out man for the mob. And I don't mind telling you, Peeper, that's what they still think. I'll start to believe it myself, if you don't quit stalling."

"You know about descriptions, Bert. They could be anybody."

"Quite right. And if I'd had to rely on descriptions I might not have been so sure. But there's another witness – and he knows you by name. So cut out the lies, and let's have the story."

"Who's your witness? How the hell does he know me."

"He's the grey-haired bloke. The one who got shot in the arm."

"Rubbish. I never saw him in my life before."

*   *   *

Permit me to draw a veil over much of the wrangling that went on for some while afterwards. Bert crowed considerably about having trapped me into an admission, but it was nothing of the sort, really. I'd always intended to admit being present – I just didn't want him to win his battles too easily. I really was surprised about the grey haired bloke, which explains why I threw my hand in when Bert mentioned him. My memory went ranging back to the days of my youth when Bert told me who the old chap was and how long he'd known me. Having stood there and seen the bloke get himself shot when all around him were petrified with fear, I already had a healthy respect for him, but now I admired him more. I'd made his life a misery, long ago, by nicking fruit out of his orchard. He'd caught me – twice – and each time let me go. Age had changed him considerably, or I'd surely have recognised him. But he'd recognised me – and in passing the word to Boggis, he hadn't mentioned what a little bastard I'd been to him over the matter of his fruit.

"How is he?" I enquired, feeling genuine concern.

"Fit as a flea. Fighting off reporters and not doing it very well. Get a paper tomorrow. His picture will be in it. And now that you've decided to see sense, Peeper, why in heaven's name didn't you contact me and pass on what you knew?"

"Because I didn't know anything."

"You knew the bloody job had happened. You knew how many were involved. You knew what they looked like. Why, hell, man – you must have known one of the sods personally."

"Rubbish. I didn't know any of those things. The job happened while I was there, but everything was confused. I didn't have time for counting. I thought I was going to be shot."

Boggis gave me a withering look.

"Some of that I can believe," he said, "because I know what a cringing little rat you are. But you saw more than you're saying, and that means you're holding out on me."

"I never saw a blind thing. Honest, Bert."

"Ah, souls. One of the blokes had his mask off for at least a couple of minutes. You must have seen his face. Who was he?"

"Oh, that. Well, I'd never seen him before in my life."

"Liar. I won't put up with this much longer." He switched on his 'no nonsense' face, which had scared me years before but which I now knew to be a load of nonsense. "I give you due warning, Peeper. You play the game with me, or I hold you on suspicion of complicity."

"Go on then. I double-dog dare you. Shove me in a cell." I sat there grinning at him until I knew I'd won. Then I went on: "Look here, Bert – why bother with me? I wasn't the only one to see his face. Why don't you leave me out of it and use the other witnesses – the staff, the other customers, the bloke who got shot?"

"Do you think I haven't tried? Nobody knows the bloke. They saw his face, they can describe him, but they don't know him."

"There you are, then. It stands to reason, you're dealing with an out of town gang. They don't know him – neither do I."

Bert subsided in his chair. He seemed almost to accept the suggestion I'd just made, and that surprised me. It wasn't the only thing that had surprised me in the last few minutes. I was very surprised to hear that Swanky Alice, the bold and renowned Alistair Proud, had bared his face in front of all those people and gone unrecognised. Behind the scenes as it were, I'd been working on that problem even as I chatted with Boggis. Thinking back, although there'd been perhaps a dozen customers in the betting shop at the time of the raid I hadn't known any of them. If they'd been local hellions the chances were high that I would have recognised them. The fact that I hadn't, made it very likely that they were ordinary, law-abiding citizens – in which case there was every chance they wouldn't have known

Proud. But that still left the counter clerks. And cashiers in betting offices make it their business to swot up on the faces and names of dubious customers for the very reason that they might get ripped off some day. A couple of the clerks had been young blokes, I remembered, and maybe if they were new, they wouldn't have had time to build up local knowledge, but one of them at least was an old stager. I'd seen him working there, off and on, for years. He must have recognised Proud, surely? And if he had, why ...?

I thought of taking that issue up with Boggis but decided against. There was a time when I used to pass everything on to him the minute I got it, but I'd burned my fingers a time or two and the pain had made me wise. Nowadays, I give Boggis whatever I think it's right for him to know – and without fail I keep a card or two back, to play against his aces when he decides to flash them.

"Just supposing I had known the bloke," I said chattily. "I could never have given you his name after what you did."

"What did I do?"

"You picked me up in front of witnesses – the worst kind of witnesses – and brought me here. Not content with that, you told them what you were picking me up for. You told them I'd been there when the job was pulled – that I was a witness."

"Course I did. But that was done to put you in the clear. All those villains watching got the message loud and clear. I was making you talk to me. there was nothing voluntary about it."

"Granted. But did I talk? That's the question they'll all be asking. Did I blab to you? Did I shop the gang? And the only way they'll ever know the answer is by watching developments. If nothing happens, they'll credit me with having stood my ground, but if you should suddenly get lucky and knock these buggers off, what are my criminal associates going to think then? They'll mark me down as a first rate squealer, and I don't have to tell you what happens to people who get that name. You backed a loser, Bert. As it happens I don't know anything, but even if I did, I wouldn't tell you."

For the past few minutes, Boggis had been growing progressively more down-hearted and despair was plain on his prune-face.

"Don't worry your rotten little head about it," he said morosely. "It isn't going to happen. I've been chasing these swines for months and the way things are looking, I'm never going to catch 'em."

"You'll catch 'em, Bert," I offered, feeling an uncharacteristic and probably misplaced stab of sympathy. "They'll make a mess of one eventually. People of that sort always do. But you won't pick 'em up through anything I can tell you – that's for sure."

       ✻   ✻   ✻

I was feeling in a much happier frame of mind next morning. When I awoke, Doreen was still snoring softly beside me and I crept out of bed without disturbing her. The morning paper was lying on the mat and I made a bee-line for it. I'm not normally an avid reader of the puerile stuff they put out as news, but I wanted to see the picture of my grey-haired benefactor – complete with arm in sling – to see if they'd done him the justice he deserved and also to have a gander at his face and figure out why I hadn't recognised him. Whether they'd published the picture or not, I never did find out. The headline on the front page hit me straight in the eye:

ARMED ROBBERY AT TOWN BETTING OFFICE

And that wasn't right — because no matter how big a robbery might be, it rarely rates banner headlines on the front page. Unless ... unless there was more to report than just details of the robbery.

I read on. There was.

Three men were in custody, helping the police with their enquiries. Their full names were given — with addresses and all — but in my book they were Swanky Alice, Bent Nelson and John Field.

FOUR

The three men were expected to appear in court that morning with a view to a remand until a suitable date of hearing. A police spokesman had hinted at possible further charges.

I wondered if the police spokesman was Bert Boggis, but somehow I didn't think so. Bert had a loud enough mouth, but he was only a detective sergeant after all, and the nick had a seemingly endless supply of beings greater than Bert. But he'd be involved in the job, somewhere up the sharp end. And if I knew him, he'd be grabbing some of the credit for the arrests. So it was a total success for Boggis, and he'd managed it without any assistance from me. I didn't know how he'd managed it, and a little bit of my mind felt pleased for him, but most of me was a mangle of shock and worry. It was well known that I'd been in a position to put the squeak in – hell, they'd gone so far as to buy me off, hadn't they? – and if there was any suggestion that the arrests had come as the result of information received ... well ... the ramifications were frightening.

Swanky Alice and his mates were in no position to hurt me. They were safely locked in separate cells and likely to stay that way. In spite of the efforts of do-gooders, bail was very seldom allowed for people on armed robbery charges. But they had friends – powerful friends – some of whom I knew and some I didn't. You can say what you like about unknown quantities, but even the ones I knew were bad enough to put the fear of God up me. They wouldn't want to know whether I was innocent or not – they'd assume I was guilty, punish me accordingly, and then offer me an *oops, sorry*, when they proved to be wrong. Maybe they wouldn't even offer me that much.

My head swimming with dark thoughts I took Doreen a cup of tea. She sat up, dreamy eyed, and flashed me a sweet smile of gratitude. *Enjoy it, love*, I advised her soundlessly. *There may not be many more where that came from. Thank your lucky stars we never got married or you might be on the verge of becoming a widow.*

I didn't say anything, because I always try to avoid burdening Doreen with my troubles. She shares the proceeds, she has an idea that I'm some sort of hush-hush operator and very occasionally she's even found herself tangled up in the fringes, but she knows very little of what I actually do, and I mean to keep it that way.

If you're asking, as I've little doubt you are, I can't explain why I'm still a single man. Doreen is the reason why I'll never marry Stella, but the answer to 'why don't I marry Doreen?' is less clear cut. It isn't because she won't have me – hell, we've lived together longer than most married couples – and it certainly isn't because I hope to meet somebody more attractive, because such a person has never been born. Being as honest as I can be, I suppose it's pure selfishness on my part. I'm not missing out on anything – and to be fair, neither is Doreen – so why should I bother tying knots? If we ever had children – and we don't particularly try to avoid them – I'd have her round to the preacher like a shot, and since I'm having a soul-baring session let me admit that she could throw a noose round me even more easily. All she has to do is issue an ultimatum – no more hanky panky this side of wedding bells – and I'll fold without a murmur. Only please don't tell her that. I'd much rather bat along as we are for as long as I can.

Doreen's a doll. I mean now, today, right at this minute. When I first met her she was a much younger doll – sweet as a nut and fresh as parsley – but now she's an older doll and I like her better than ever. I've heard tell of people growing old gracefully and I don't really know what that means, but when Doreen starts to grow old – which won't happen for a long time yet – I expect I shall understand the term better. It's even possible that one day she'll become less attractive sexually, but I don't worry my head about that. If it ever comes about I shall already have died – of old age.

The house we live in is a neat little terraced job within a cough and spit of the posh part of the town. Doreen owns it and I'm her permanent lodger with home comforts. Across the street from us there are some very up-market detached jobs with twin garages, sun-lounges, extensive garden and – in one or two cases – even swimming pools. Doreen would love to move across there, and I've promised to buy her something in that class the minute my ship comes in, but it's a long time coming.

On the day in question I wasn't thinking about ships. If I had been, I'd have given nothing for the chances of mine ever coming in. But I had no intention of going down without a struggle, so as soon as I'd seen Doreen on her way to up I made excuses and set off in search of Boggis.

You can never be sure with Bert Boggis. Sometimes when you want him – and particularly if you want him urgently – he seems to have disappeared off the face of the earth. Other times you only have to think of his name and there he is, standing at your elbow. Today he was easy enough to find, but not easy to talk to. Normally, when I ask him to meet me, he agrees without too much trouble, but today he was far too busy and couldn't possibly see me before a week the following Tuesday. I had to drop him a hint that I knew something good. It was completely false, but predictably it worked like a charm. Half an hour later I was sitting in his car, parked up a back crack by the river.

"Go on – let's have it," he said.

"How did you manage to touch for Swanky Alice and his mates?"

"Never mind that. What have you got to tell me?"

"Bugger all, Bert. But I need to know what happened."

"Yes, but just a minute. I thought you had something to pass on. A useful little snippet, you said. Something that was going to please me."

There was disbelief in his face and I watched it change to petulance. I hadn't a shred of sympathy for him. In fact, I came nearer to hating him at that moment than I ever come most of the time.

"You selfish bloody pig," I said with feeling. "You engineer me into deep trouble, then you won't even see me to discuss it. I could be rubbed out, minced and sold for dog meat and you wouldn't give a bugger. You're a shithouse, Bert. A proper one. Every time I …"

"Will you tell me what the hell you're babbling about?"

"The Crewe job – as you very well know. You make a public show of dragging me in as a witness, then, just a few hours later, you just happen to arrest the gang. Now where the hell does that leave me?"

"Christ! Is there no end to your stupidity?" He tried to say it loftily, with a sneer on his face, but the sneer was bogus.

"You're the one who's being stupid, Bert. You've exposed me. Stuck me out on a limb. And now I'm coming to you for protection."

"Protection? You don't need any bloody protection. We got the gen on the Crewe job from a totally different source."

"I'd thank you for telling me, Bert, if I didn't know already. The point is – you know it and so do I, but do Swanky Alice's mates know it? I don't mean Nelson and Field – I mean the buggers outside."

"What difference does it make? Why should they blame you?"

"Because they ... because they know you had me as a witness."

I'd been obliged to stumble at that stage, because my brain was working faster than my tongue. Maybe twenty-five percent of the blame I was laying on Boggis was unjust. He didn't know about the hundred quid tongue-locker. But he sure as hell knew that there were grounds on which the ungodly could suspect me of informing – and he also knew that he'd placed me in that predicament. He had the grace to relent.

"Look, Peeper. I can see the way it turned out was a bit unfortunate, but don't you think you're making too much of it? After all, they can only suspect. There's no way they can know for sure."

"That's true, but it isn't much comfort. These people are not like you, Bert. They don't have to prove anything. They only have to think it – and that's enough to justify all sorts of mayhem."

Boggis shook his head – and I'd have said he wasn't faking.

"You're jumping at bogeymen, Peeper. Nothing's going to happen to you. And anyway, if they start to harass you, you can always ring the station and make a complaint."

"Shall I ask for you by name, Bert?"

"Hell, no. Don't do that. That might give the wrong impression."

＊   ＊   ＊

Bumping along in the back of Lenny Bethel's car, with Chester Moreland sitting on one side and Big Ginger Fish on the other, I had plenty of time to consider the utter futility of the advice I'd had from Boggis. Due to the speed with which I found myself in my present position, ringing the nick had been impossible beforehand. Later would be too late to save me harassment. There might not be a later.

No, you haven't turned over two pages. It's just that I like to leap ahead and list an event so that I can go back and describe how it came to happen. This is also my way of saying, *I told you so*, to anyone who – like Detective Sergeant Albert Boggis – might have thought I was mad to go in fear of retribution.

The invitation to a motor trip came within the hour after my little chat with Boggis. I'd skirted around town centre, keeping to the by-ways and dodging shadows, but to get to the Albion Hotel which was my destination I had to cross Market Street at some point. I don't know whether the sods had been following me, or whether it was sheer chance that brought the big Rover to the right place at the right time, but I'd hardly taken a dozen paces along the pavement before the car was alongside and the open rear door beckoned.

You can say, 'No thanks, I'd rather walk," you can

turn quickly and hurry away, you can even scream blue murder if that takes your fancy, but you can't avoid that sort of summons in the long run. And if you do show resistance you worsen the situation. They might have to leave you alone this time but the bill doubles – and when they finally catch up with you, it all comes out of your hide.

So I bowed to the inevitable, climbed in and let them spirit me away. Not cowardice this, but common sense. Whatever they had planned for me I hoped to talk my way out of it, one way or another, and the best way to start off on a chat defence is to play ball.

I hadn't a clue where they were taking me and I didn't bother asking. I didn't grumble or protest. I just sat there, dwarfed by Messrs Moreland and Fish, and waited to see what the future brought. All very calm and composed – and so I was, on the outside. Inside, I seethed with a thousand fears and a single question. The fears would have to wait to be realised, but maybe I could do something about the question, which was simply, *for whom are these heavy sods working?* More often than not, if you give me the name of a local bruiser I'll tell you who he works for, but at the time I speak of, the criminal hierarchy in town was in a state of flux. Bethel and Fish, I knew, had been part of the Frenchy Watts mob, but Frenchy had been inside for some time – no small thanks to my own efforts – and they must have found a new master. Chester Moreland (Eric Moreland really, but a native of Chester and so called to avoid confusion with another Eric Moreland locally) had once been a switch-car driver for Stevie Brooks, until Stevie also had been put out of circulation. So I was left in considerable doubt. Both the Watts mob and the Brooks mob were still functioning on a much reduced scale, but whether these three now worked for one, or the other, or a third mob unknown to me, was a question that would only be answered when I got to wherever they were taking me.

I fell to considering the new supplementary question and at once began to regret it. If I wished to know which direction we were heading all I had to do was glance through the window and follow the passing scene, familiar to me since boyhood. True there was the high shoulder of Chester Moreland limiting my view to the left and the bulging chest of Big Ginger Fish blocking out part of the right hand window, but I could see enough to know that we were climbing out of town, along Meadow Range, towards the Sephton Park Estate. Sephton Park runs for miles, forming a curved wedge like a giant banana round the north side of town. All the rich people live there, their reason being that all the big, posh, detached houses have been built there, and most of the big time crooks live there too, their reason being because they happen to be rich.

The realisation that we were heading for Sephton Park came as no surprise and caused no alarm, but *the fact that this knowledge was not being concealed from me* seemed very ominous indeed. I don't know why the possession of a vivid imagination is supposed to be such an asset. Mine's as vivid as hell. I'm always conjuring up pictures of the most unpleasant kind. So all my imagination does for me is scare the shit out of me. I'd begun this ride expecting to be put through somebody's mill in reprisal for an offence of which I was totally innocent – namely the shopping of Swanky Alice, Bent Newton and John Field – and I'd accepted as inevitable a certain amount of pain and suffering. But these buggers were being far too open about it. Far from tying me up and bundling me in the boot, they were letting me see exactly where we were going, as though they didn't give a damn. Maybe they had no reason to care – because I was destined only for a polite wigging. Maybe they felt confident that I'd be too scared to talk afterwards? Or maybe – and this was the worrying thought – they knew I wouldn't talk afterwards because I was travelling on what the Yanks used to call a 'one-way ticket'?

I ask you to remember that up to this stage, nothing of great importance had been said. I'd said nothing at all. Lenny Bethel had several times offered to perform certain prohibited sexual acts on the drivers of cars that got in his way. Chester Moreland had told Big Ginger a very unfunny joke and Big Ginger had mentioned the number of pints of bitter beer he'd drunk the night before. That apart, silence had reigned, so I can hardly claim to have been subjected to threats, but before the journey was over I could feel myself quivering like blancmange and my past evil deeds were parading before my eyes.

We turned into the drive of a house, and recognition of the place almost shocked me out of my shock. I'd been here before – more than once. In particular, I could remember a highly entertaining half hour I'd spent, hiding in those big rhododendrons on the right.(*) But knowing the house was one thing – it didn't give much of a lead on the identity of whoever had sent for me.

They wheeled me in through familiar doors and into a familiar hall, then along a familiar corridor into a familiar office. There was a man sitting at a desk in the office – a smallish man, but very smartly dressed and groomed. I stared at him wide eyed. He wasn't in the least familiar. The man smiled pleasantly at me, but his

(*) See 'GRASS'S FANCY'

remark was plainly addressed to his hirelings.

"What does he say for himself?"

"Nothing, boss," Big Ginger offered. "Jeez, you never heard nobody say nothing the way Peeper does – ain't that right, Peeper?"

I grinned foolishly. I had nothing special to say.

"He's too comfortable," the man said. "Make him uncomfortable."

Hands gripped me. One by the scruff of the neck, another by the crutch and several more by the arms and head. There seemed to be hands all over the place, and as though working in concert they all started pressing inwards in a determined attempt to come together somewhere in the middle of my spine. The pain was excruciating. I was forced to break my personal rule about not using obscene language.

"You copulating, secretly registered parlourmaids' mistakes" I screamed. "You performing male genitalia. You places of bowel relief."

The pain was mercifully brief, and when it stopped, I stopped. The dapper little man smiled at me. His smile was warm – genuine.

"You really shouldn't have – should you?" he said.

"Shouldn't have what – for Christ's sake?"

"You had a little whisper to the cops."

"Bullshit. I did nothing of the sort."

"He's much too comfortable," the man said. The smile had gone from his face and he seemed to be waiting for something important to happen. So was I, and neither of us was disappointed. The hands swooped in again to take my arms where they were never designed to go, but it was the knee that did most damage, coming up from somewhere near the floor to find the only natural fork apart from my armpits and raise me by something like a foot. I didn't swear. I might have screamed – in fact I'm pretty sure I did scream – but that was just the wind being driven out of me. The only thing I did deliberately was die. Death came as a merciful release.

But I came to life again – and I was lying on the floor. I remember thinking what a nice carpet lay against my face and what good taste the little man must have. Then it occurred to me that I had no feeling in my arms. After that, as memory returned, I started worrying like hell about the state of my wedding tackle. The feeling I had in that region was a sort of empty one – as though there was nothing there any longer – but after a minute or so it started to hurt like mad. I was grateful for the pain. If they were hurting, at least I still had them. I turned my head carefully making no attempt to lift it. The three bruisers were standing round me in a half ring and the little man was leaning forward over the desk, looking down. I could only see his face. It was smiling.

"Call the dogs off," I said. "Damn you, whoever you are. How the hell can I explain if these knuckleheads won't let me."

"Get up, Peeper," he invited.

"Knackers. These pigs of yours'll knock me down again."

"They will if you keep calling them nasty names."

"Well, Christ, man. What do you expect. No explanations, just the boot in as far as it'll go. You expect me to like it? A man takes a thumping, he wants to know what it's for."

"You know perfectly well what it's for."

"Balls. I haven't a clue. I never put a foot wrong."

"You're mumbling, Peeper. I can't hear a word. Get up."

"No thanks. I'm a lot happier where I aaaaaaam."

I finished on an elongated note and I also finished on my feet. Chester Moreland had lifted me by the hair. He kept his grip on my tearing scalp and I hung there like a rag doll.

"You witnessed certain events at the Crewe betting shop," the man said. "You were paid to keep your trap shut. You took the money."

"I hadn't much choice, had I? But who wants your bloody money? You can have it back any time you like. Look, I … I … I …"

When somebody tries to put your left hand against the nape of your neck you have little choice but to stand on tippy toes. Also it's rather hard to keep talking. I stopped talking.

"You were put on trust," the little man said. "You betrayed that trust. You went squealing to the cops."

"I never told the cops a blind thing."

"You were seen. You were talking to that man … what's his name?"

"Boggis," Lenny Bethel offered. "Detective Sergeant Boggis."

"That bastard!" I made to spit on the carpet but thought better of it. "He dragged me in off the street. He threatened to charge me. He said I was tied up with the gang. Boggis is a shithouse."

"And under pressure, you named names?" the small man said gently.

"Not even my own bloody name. I wouldn't tell Boggis if he had a snake crawling up his arse. I told him nothing. Nothing!"

For a minute I thought I'd won a round. The small man had a frown on his face and I thought, since his smile had proved to be poison, maybe his frown meant sympathy. He swapped looks with his thugs, then spoke to me in an odd, wheedling way.

"Come on, Peeper. What do you expect me to
think? You were there when the job was pulled. You
had a session with this bloody policeman, whatever his
name is, and next minute John and the boys have been
lifted. Who squawked if you didn't? You're surely not
suggesting it was John Field, or Nelson, or Proud?"

"Hell, no. They've all been locked up. It's in the
papers."

"Of course. They wouldn't shop themselves. So who
else could it have been? It must have been you,
Peeper."

I had a brainwave about that time – at any rate, it
seemed to be a brainwave when I first had it.

"You're forgetting something aren't you?" I said,
feeling triumphant. "The cops only knocked off three –
so what happened to number four? There had to be
four men, hadn't there? Otherwise, Field and his
mates would have had to walk home. There's your
squealer, my friend. Not me at all, but the bloke who
drove the getaway car."

My triumph was short lived. Out of the corner of my
eye I saw Lenny Bethel make a big fist and start it on its
way. I hadn't time to duck. I finished up in the corner
of the room, my face feeling as though it had been
shattered into a thousand pieces.

"What the hell was that for?" I mumbled.

"Lenny drove the getaway car," the small man said
sweetly.

*   *   *

"Take him out," the small man said, "and put him
in the car."

I didn't know whether to be relieved or terrified.
They'd been working on me for quite a while and I'd

lost count of how many bones they'd broken. I was still
sticking to my story – hell, it was the truth, so I had to
stick to it – but I'd failed to win any of them over.
When I saw Bethel and Moreland join the small man
and retreat into a corner of the office for a whispered
chinwag I still had enough life left in me to wonder
what they were discussing, but there was no way I
could go and listen. Big Ginger Fish kept a tight hold
on me. When they came back and my removal was
ordered, I hadn't the slightest idea what it signified.
But it didn't matter either way. He wanted me placed in
the car, to the car I would freely go. If they meant to
free me – or kill me – so be it. I decided to be relieved
and terrified alternately, by numbers.

It was the same car – a rather nice black Rover – and
I was allotted my usual place, between Fish and
Moreland on the back seat. Lenny Bethel took the
wheel again and I was surprised to see the small man
climb into the front passenger seat. Whatever he had in
mind for me, he intended to witness it, or so it seemed.
My curiosity suddenly became very sharp. In lieu of a
hearty breakfast, the condemned man felt the urge to
ask a question.

"I'm afraid I've forgotten your name," I told the
small man.

"Don't worry about it, you won't need it," he
smiled.

"I always thought that house belonged to Frenchy
Watts," I persisted.

"Frenchy's on holiday," he said. "I'm renting the
place."

"Does Frenchy know about it?"

The question was insulting if taken in a certain way,
and the way I said it was calculated to insult him. The

small man didn't move, but he flashed a look to Big Ginger Fish, who thumped me hard in the ribs. I was past caring. They couldn't hurt me any more.

"Why don't you fight your own battles, you cowardly little turd?" I asked the small man. "If I had you on your own, I'd ..."

And this time it wasn't physical interference that cut me off in mid-sentence. It was sound. Terrible sound. Beautiful sound. I couldn't believe it myself, and certainly the others couldn't. If I could hear one two-tone horn I could hear a dozen. And there were blue lights flashing, nearing, converging. Bethel had driven the Rover as far as the end of the drive, but its nose was barely showing in the street when there were police cars on all sides. Everybody in the Rover sat tight. Around us, doors were springing open and men in blue pouring out. A uniformed inspector was first to arrive at the Rover, but he had plenty of back-up right there with him.

"You Leonard Bethel?" he asked the driver.

"Yes. What's the ..."

"I have a warrant for your arrest."

"What the hell for?"

"Robbery. Handling stolen goods." He stuck his head in at the door and glared at Big Ginger. "You Harold Fish?"

"That's right."

"I've got one for you, too. Same charges. You Eric Moreland?"

"That's me."

"Yours is just for handling. But don't worry, we'll think of something else." The Inspector ducked out of the car, walked round and opened the front passenger door. He glared at the small man. "And you must be

Peter David Parrott," he accused.

"Look, what's this all about, officer?" the small man said. "If you've got warrants to arrest my men, you must have your reasons, but I don't see how that affects me. If you want to …"

"Are you Parrott?" the inspector said.

"That is my name, but …"

"I have a warrant for your arrest. Handling stolen goods. I also have a warrant to search this house and I'm going to do that right now – in your presence." He turned his back on the Rover and shouted, "Right, lads. Take 'em and put 'em somewhere safe. All except this little chap. He stays with me."

*　　*　　*

Let me be the first to admit, I enjoyed every minute of it. I even enjoyed the events which followed and which affected me in a more personal way. The inspector ignored me completely until he had cleared the others from the Rover, then he leaned in and gave me a most unfriendly look.

"Name and address?" He snapped. I told him.

"Is that straight? You wouldn't be kidding me?"

"That's straight up."

"Right. We'll see about that."

"He used his personal radio, but he stood far enough away to prevent me picking up his conversation. After a few minutes he came back. He didn't look a lot more friendly.

"I don't like it," he confided. "Hanging about with a shower like this, I'd knock you off for conspiracy. But I've checked at Headquarters and they won't back me. Your Guardian Angel must be working overtime. So

I'm letting you go for now, and I don't want to see you ever again. Now piss off, before I change my mind."

* * *

"Parrott!" I thought, as I was walking home. "Parrott. No wonder the bugger wouldn't give me his name."

FIVE

The joy of unexpected release when the brain has told the body that all is lost can be a very heady thing. I forgot my aches and my budding bruises, managed to walk normally when little voices in my head suggested the advantages of a bow-legged gait and even – when passing two girls so much too young for me that I ought to have been ashamed – convinced myself that potency was still an asset.

I particularly liked what had happened to Peter David Parrott.

Parrott had sneaked in under my radar screen somehow. I didn't think he could possibly have been long in the area, or my scouts would have drawn him to my attention at an earlier stage. But he wasn't a new criminal in any other sense of the word. He had authority – I could almost say *charisma* but I had no wish to soil that word – and the sort of experience that must have come from bossing some other outfit in some other town. How he'd managed to move in and take over established territory I couldn't imagine, but I guessed there was a Frenchy connection somewhere. Frenchy Watts had been in prison for some time and was likely to remain there for a while yet, so the chances were high that his organisation had been sophisticated enough to import a new director. Heaven alone knew what might have happened if – ten years from now – Frenchy had returned to find King Parrott firmly established on his throne, but the point was academic after today's little development. At any rate, it would be academic if the cops managed to stitch Parrott for something good. All this left me with another thought hanging. *The king is dead – long live the king.* I'd have to set my stall out and discover, as quickly as possible, what contingency plans might exist for the crowning of a new king.

But I'd worry about that some other time. For the moment it was enough that I was free as air and kindly fate had frowned on my enemies. They'd all had a go at me, Bethel, Moreland and Fish with their horrid, knobbly bodies and Parrott, vicariously, by issuing his directives, so it was intensely satisfying to know that a substantial form of come-uppance was about to be visited on them. In some ways it would have been nicer if I could have done it myself – if I could have taken them on one at a time and beaten the shit out of them – but Parrott would have been clever enough to avoid letting me catch him on his own, and each of the other three could have snapped me like a match stalk between his fingers, so I wasted no time in day dreaming. The cops would do it for me. My troubles were over. Life was great.

My euphoria lasted till I was half-way home.

Aches and bruises are remarkable things. Great joy seems to drive them away, but despair brings them galloping back. From the minute I realised that my head was still in a noose the whole circumference of that important member began to throb with pain. It developed insupportable heaviness that threatened to leave me with permanent curvature of the spine. The cuts on my lips began to smart with new vigour, my shoulders grew to twice their normal size, my knees separated by at least a foot and when a most fragrant piece of young skirt went swishing by I was conscious of very limited arousal.

Far from having ended my troubles, the police raid on the Parrott gang had served to increase them. The raid had been fortuitous, but what could have sparked it off? Clearly, somebody had blown the whistle on Peter David Parrott – not for his puny assault on me, which wouldn't have rated two lines in the local rag, but for honest-to-God skullduggery tied up with the recent spate of robberies. The plain truth – that I had known nothing about his connection with those crimes and couldn't possibly have informed on him – was as valueless as plain truth so often is. Swanky Alice's friends had gone for me – now *their* friends (Peter David Parrott's friends) would go for me in turn. And it was the sort of paper chase that had no visible end. By this time, with seven of their best members incarcerated at the nick, the whole criminal fraternity would be screaming for the head of whoever was blowing the gaff – and until they discovered otherwise they'd be happy to believe it was me. I began to hope like hell that they'd find out who was doing it. It was very much in my own interests that they should. Hell, it went even deeper than that. For professional reasons, I needed the information too. And on top of all that, I was becoming very curious indeed.

* * *

Domestic problems loomed small against all the weight of my other worries, but small or not they had to be solved. I was doing my best to work out whether I should go home – to Doreen – and hole up there until the heat died down, or whether I should first call on

Stella, give her the usual attention and leave her in happy enough mood to manage without me for a day or two, when I paid an unexpected and completely unplanned visit to the Golden Roof Restaurant.

Fate, rather than the attractions of Vince Skinner and his wares, caused me to turn in at that door. I was passing the place only because it lay on my route, and my intention was to walk on by, but as the caff door hove in sight I saw a familiar threesome approaching from the opposite direction. They were Fred Head, Cutter Watson and Smithy. For the record, Smithy's name is James Smith, and in spite of the common nature of the surname there's only one 'Smithy' in town. Cutter Watson was christened Harold Gavin, but his skill with tin-snips on church roofs and up electricity pylons has caused his given names to become redundant. And as for Fred Head, well believe it or not, that's nearly his proper name. Lazy folk have abbreviated him to his present handle from Fred Hedley. Anyway, these were the three who appeared before me, and bearing in mind what I'd been thinking about immediately prior to meeting them, I naturally assumed they'd be on the look-out for me. So I put a brave face on, marched boldly up to them and offered a friendly "how do?"

"Hiya, Peeper," Fred Head said.

"Hello, mate," Smithy said.

"Coming in for a cuppa?" Cutter Watson invited.

No sign of animosity from any of them. You'll have heard the story of the farmer who sets off to borrow a tractor from the chap on the next farm? On the way, he starts to imagine reasons why the other farmer might refuse the loan – and he gets so worked up about this that the minute he meets the other farmer he tells him he can stuff the bloody tractor up his jumper.

That's the way I felt. I'd carefully worked out how everybody would be after my blood, and when they weren't, well, I almost forgot how to handle it. So I stumbled and mumbled and finished up at a table for four, in the caff, with Fred Head buying me a coffee.

A lot of odd things were happening all at once. It was odd, to begin with, for me to be taking beverage with this crowd. I'd met them often enough, exchanged pleasantries, even stood next to them in a pub and swigged the odd pint, but somehow the occasion to sit with them at a table in a restaurant had never arisen before. Generally speaking, only cronies sit at the same table, and I was anything but a crony. But somehow, it happened, and but for the timing it would have seemed quite natural. The timing though, left me with the scrag end of a suspicion. Maybe they were gunning for me after all? Maybe this show of mateyness was just the bait and it covered a sharp hook poised to slash itself into gullible old me? I played the conversation with that thought in mind, but after ten minutes I convinced myself that I'd got it wrong. They certainly weren't trying to talk me into anything. In fact, the conversation verged on the edge of being a total bore. A few recent dog-races were re-run, Smithy's slatterny wife was slandered, Skinner's products (inevitably) were damned for their tastelessness and mystery content and one or two dirty jokes, all so old I'd heard them in my cradle, were bandied about. If this small team of hicks had any designs on me – if they were trying to scare me or trap me into admissions – then every man-jack of 'em was 'Oscar' material.

When I left the table to order and pay for four more cups of Skinner's essence I was really only trying to get away from the sheer banality of the chat. The idea that

I might have moved deliberately, having foreknowledge of what was about to happen, should be dismissed as false, but looking back on the occasion I have to admit it could easily have looked that way. I didn't even hear the door open, being mesmerised by the smell, the steam and Skinner's sleight of hand, and when I turned back towards the table – they were standing there.

Two jacks – both of them too smart, too young to be Boggis. How did I know they were jacks, then? Well, you develop a nose for that sort of thing. But I'm not being completely frank when I say that. The truth is, I recognised Detective Constable Jack Coughlin straight off and I knew the other's face from somewhere. A moment's thought reminded me that it was Detective Constable Ivor Moore.

"Hello Smithy, hello Fred," Coughlin said.

"You got a coat somewhere, Cutter?" Moore enquired.

"What do I want a coat for?" Cutter Watson said, looking sour.

"In case it rains," Moore explained. "I shouldn't want you to get wet walking to the car."

"You too, Smithy," Coughlin added. "Get your coat on."

"I ain't got a bloody coat," Smithy grumbled.

"No matter then. You'll do as you are. Come on, let's have you."

"Hang on a minute," Fred Head said. "What's all this about."

"Not you, Fred," Coughlin said. "It's just your mates this time. But don't lose heart, old son. One of these days you'll get lucky."

"You haven't said what you're taking us for," Smithy pointed out.

"Haven't we, Smithy?" Coughlin said with a broad grin. "Shall we say robbery to be going on with? We'll sort it out at the nick."

"Robbery? What the hell are you talking about? What robbery?"

"Mortley Road Post Office, Gordon Good's Wines. Take your pick."

"I know nowt about those jobs. Neither does Cutter."

"That's what they all say, Smithy. They all say that."

* * *

They left in procession, with Vince Skinner, Fred Head and me gawping after them. I was astounded. I'd just watched history in the making and I didn't feel I could let the moment pass without comment.

"I don't think that's ever happened before, Vince," I said.

"What's that, Peeper?"

"The cops coming in here and snatching your customers."

"Very rare, very rare," Skinner agreed with a safe nod. "But not unknown, Peeper – not by any means. Something's happening in this town. That's the second time this afternoon."

"They've been in before, you say?"

"Not the same two. It was that bastard Boggis and another of his mates. They came in after lunch and lifted Jim and Tony Gates."

"Did they, by God. What was it about?"

"Nothing said, mate. Just up and out. But I don't like it."

Fred Head had risen and walked over to join us. He wore the look of a very puzzled man. Watching his

arrival, those litle pin-pricks of fear began to assail me
again. *They think I fixed it*, my fevered brain told me.
*They think I lured them in here so that the cops could pluck 'em
like daisies.*

"I don't like it either," Fred said. "You're right
about that, Vince, there's something bloody odd afoot.
I wouldn't give a damn if it wasn't so flaming
embarrassing."

"Embarrassing?" Great minds thinking alike, Vince
Skinner and I used the same word simultaneously. It
had sounded so odd, coming from Fred Head, that
neither of us could believe it. Fred nodded.

"Embarrassing – that's what I said. And so it is. The
buggers come in here, grab Cutter and Smithy and
wheel 'em away. But they don't bother with me. I'm
left hanging round like a spare one. What the hell am I
supposed to think? It's bloody embarrassing."

I was intensely relieved by Fred's total lack of enmity
towards me. I was also ever so slightly amazed by it.
Having convinced myself that every crook in town had
my name right at the top of his hate list it was hard to
imagine that these three hadn't heard of my supposed
treachery. But it was obvious they hadn't. Lord, if
they'd had the slightest suspicion about me, my purely
accidental departure from their table at the precise
moment when the axe was about to fall would have
clinched my guilt in their minds. My relief was such that
I hung on in Vince Skinner's place a lot longer than I
intended. For about half an hour I sat with Fred Head,
commiserating with him while I flooded my belly with
sloppy coffee. After that the door opened again and
Detective Constable Moore leaned in.

"Come on, Fred," he shouted. "We've got
something for you now."

Fred Head seemed pleased to go. I watched the
worry lines fall from his brow as he strutted to the door

to join Moore and be spirited away to the nick. He grinned at Skinner and me as he went out.

"What's the bloody world coming to, Vince?" I wondered.

"Damned if I know, Peeper, but it's bad. I'm going to complain about this to the Chief Constable. The way these buggers are going at the moment, I'll soon have no customers left."

SIX

During the next few days I wandered round the place in a state of full-time unease, as though nuclear war had been declared and I was waiting to see the mushrooms start sprouting. What made the whole thing more eerie was that everybody in town seemed to have been bitten by the same bug. Not just Doreen, who seemed to get quite stroppy at the slightest provocation, or Stella, who had seldom welcomed me with less show, but all the people I passed in the street, or boozed with, or bought fags from, or stood with at bus stops.

Some of this was in my own mind, but not all of it, and it seemed likely to me that increased police activity was one important underlying cause. I became an avid reader of newspapers and the clues turned up daily on the printed page. Clutch after clutch of rogues appeared before the local magistrates, to be remanded for trial and kept in custody. The population thinned out perceptibly and I spent some anxious hours puzzling about the corollary, which had to be that the cell block at the town nick was bursting at the seams. I'm no stranger to that cell block. I didn't think it could possibly cope with the number of people currently being lodged there by the court. They must have had to build an annexe – or maybe Boggis had lost his office in the cause of prisoner accommodation.

The real answer, I supposed, was that they were shipping 'em to and from prison on a day-to-day basis.

And I didn't much care about that, to be perfectly honest. What I did care about – very strongly – was my lack of knowledge about this strange blight that had suddenly affected the town, and that threatened my own livelihood in a very material way. How the hell could an honest grass flourish in a place where the police were fixing to clear up every crime – and lock up every criminal – in the entire district without any help from the said grass? Much more of this and I'd be redundant, tossed on the scrap heap, and somehow I couldn't picture a grateful Boggis making an impassioned speech and shoving over a golden handshake.

I did my damnedest to contact Boggis and get the truth, but I was peeing in the wind. Whenever I rang the nick they refused to put me through to him on the grounds that he was unable to deal with outside calls and had had his extension temporarily disconnected. I tried leaving messages in one or other of the soppy codes we'd devised, then waiting for him in remembered places, but he simply never showed up. Finally, in desperation, I rang his wife at their home number – and that was almost a complete waste of time too.

Not a complete waste of time though. Even in the midst of all my trouble I never fail to enjoy a quick chat over the phone with Jenny Boggis. As a deliberate matter of policy, we've never met each other, but she knows who I am and we often talk. I tell you the stuff she breathes over the line is the most modest, proper and discreet stuff – but if I could bottle it and sell it, I'd make a fortune. Jenny is as pretty as Bert is ugly – as kind hearted as he is a swine – as sensible as he is stupid and as helpful as he is obstructive. The truest thought ever uttered is the one that goes, *opposites attract*. It has to be true, or Jenny couldn't possibly have married Albert Boggis, borne him some splendid kids and kept up the pretence that she thinks the world of him.

But for a very rare once, Jenny had no help to offer – unless you could say that by moving my mind from the general to the particular, she helped a little. None of these impersonal barriers from Jenny. She explained to me, point blank, that Bert had no intention of speaking to me for the present. He wanted me out of his hair. I was an embarrassment to him. He didn't want me to come out from under my rotten log and he wouldn't be held responsible for the consequences if I did. Jenny Boggis didn't put it quite that way, of course. Not having an ounce of cruelty in her, she explained it all very kindly – but the meaning was the same, and I knew I had to forget about Bert Boggis as a source of aid. It's no use pretending I wasn't sore about it. Hell, I was sore enough to kick the selfish swine in the crutch if I'd had him handy, but I gave Jenny a mild, sweet *thank-you* and hung up hard enough to put the telephone handset at risk.

But for one thing I was very grateful – the heat seemed to have gone right off me. It was as though the message had gone out to lay off Peeper, because Peeper wasn't to blame. Of the few active crooks still left in town, none had their knives in me, although I ran into most of them one way or another, during that unsettled period. The current attitude was at such variance with the one that had appertained earlier that I needed to put some work into reasoning it out. No doubt about those early contacts with Swanky Alice, Bent Nelson and John Field, or the subsequent run-in with Peter David Parrott and his hangers-on. They'd hated my guts because they believed in my guilt. It was possible (wasn't it?) that stories about how I'd run squealing to the cops had only had limited circulation, and that the people I'd supposedly informed against were all in custody and out of the way. But I couldn't believe that my fame wouldn't have spread further. Thieves and rogues do tend to hang together in adversity. If the surviving mobs had heard the story that all these arrests of other mobsters had come about through Peeper's perfidy, they'd have ganged together and gone for me, even though I'd never harmed them.

So, in some way that I couldn't figure out, great minds had changed their tune and the 'all clear' had been sounded on me. That being so, another question reared its head – a question to which I didn't know the answer *but the big boys did*. Somebody, other than the wretched Peeper, had gone to the cops and blown the gaff.

Whoever he was – he had to be a big one.

Well, consider the alternatives. If you take me as the first example, I could never have put in so much high grade information on so many of the top people in such a short time. The reason why is probably very plain, but just in case it isn't, let me explain. I don't run with the gangs. If I did, and Bert Boggis caught me at it, I'd finish up in the cells alongside the rest. What I do is stay on the fringe of things, prod a finger in here and a finger in there and have a lick at whatever sticks to my fingers. If the taste is right, I pass the recipe to Bert Boggis and he does the rest. I do, by pure mischance, get a bit too close to criminal activities sometimes, and whenever that happens I have to wriggle myself out. But I could never become so deeply involved that I knew so much about so many – and since I don't have the information, I can't give it.

I'm far and away the best copper's snout in town. Call me all the big-headed twits you can lay your tongue to, but when you've finished, listen to what I say. If there was another (or maybe more than one other) in the same class as myself, he or they'd be handicapped in the same way as I am. So whoever was responsible for the upheaval the town was currently experiencing, it certainly wasn't another bloke in the same game as myself.

No – even if you don't follow my argument, take my word for it that whoever was turning in the crooks *had to be a crook himself.* An active crook, I mean. And as I said a little earlier, he had to be a big one. Because a little crook can blow the gaff on the stuff he's been involved in and the names of his immediate circle of fellow crooks – but to blow the gaff on half the town he has to be big, big, big.

These were the thoughts that mainly occupied me during those uneasy days. Most of all, I kept asking myself who the hell could this supergrass possibly be? I couldn't come up with an inspired guess. Frankly, I couldn't think of a single person whose pedigree and background would precisely fit the frame, but I could think of a hell of a lot who *might* fit. And the problem was, I couldn't eliminate. I couldn't say, *the following have all been locked up and therefore it has to be somebody else*, because, crooks being the crafty swines they are, any one of the dozens in custody might have been the supergrass. Even Peter David Parrott? Well, why not? Parrott was a new arrival in town. Who was I to say he hadn't been sent in as a plant, to turn himself in with all his mates, then wriggle out of the reckoning through some official subterfuge?

*   *   *

In the end I gave it up and retired into my shell to play the husband at home, the fancy bloke at the Albion Hotel and the solitary boozer in a lot of pubs and clubs in town. My hours became more regular and reliable. I began to have my meals at the proper time, to watch telly in the evening and to show Doreen I hadn't forgotten the proper way to do things. Doreen was very pleased about it. There were even a few evenings when Doreen went out and I stayed in – a complete reversal of the usual set-up – and I was in no hurry to change things, since our finances were healthy enough to run at a slow chug for ages.

I say Doreen was happy about it, and she was, which makes it all the more ironical that the next events came about through Doreen's unhappiness. She'd been out to one of her keep-fit classes, something she's been interested in for years, and I was at home, knocking a bit of supper together, when she came in, rushed through to the lounge, flung herself on the sofa and started sobbing fit to burst. I've never found it easy to respond to women when they cry. The soft hand of sympathy doesn't seem to live with me. I want to tell them to snap out of it and not be so bloody childish. I almost followed those lines with Doreen, but something about her sobbing held me back. It seemed dreadfully genuine, not the sort women often put on to promote sympathy. So I went and sat alongside her, put a hand on her shoulder, and a voice that didn't sound in the least like mine asked her what was the matter.

"It was horrible, horrible," she said. "And we couldn't do anything to stop it. We just stood there, helpless, and watched it happen. If only we could have done something, somehow …"

"That's not making a lot of sense, kid," I pointed out.

"They took her right in front of us," she said.

"Look, Doreen. Get a hold of yourself. Who the hell are you talking about. Who's *her?* Who's *they?* What happened for God's sake?"

"And she's pregnant too. You can see she is. She's plump already and you can see it swelling up. She wasn't going to come much longer. She was going to leave off coming till after the baby."

The trouble with Doreen is that she always assumes too much. She mentions a person and expects you to know that person – or an event and expects you to know the background – and if you don't cotton on she tends to get quite excited about it and to make unfair references to your mental capacity. There was a great deal more conversation between us before I got at the truth – I reckon it took me at least half an hour to bottom it – and I won't bore you with a transcript.

It appeared that a local lady called Bernadette O'Mahoney had been taken away by force from the local health centre at which Doreen's health classes were held. Mrs. O'Mahoney had succumbed to nature's laws and was podding up very nicely, but as long as the black wool tights would fit her she had carried on with the keep-fit exercises. Today, half-way through the session, a couple of strange men had entered the hall, laid hands on Bernadette and carried her, kicking, struggling and swearing in bog-Irish, out of the health centre and away. It had happened too quickly for anyone to prevent it. All the other sweaty ladies had gazed at the scene in horror, then fallen to gabbling amongst themselves about the inhumanity of it all. Most had been too self-conscious to take up the chase, for that would have exposed them to public gaze in all their body-stockinged near-nakedness, and the few hardy souls who had overcome pride sufficiently to follow, had done so too late.

But the police had been called. A sergeant and a constable, both in uniform, had stood in the middle of a great bunch of hot, chattering women and taken down details of the occurrence. They had not seemed unduly concerned (showed typical male bloody arrogance and lack of common decency to women, as Doreen put it) and after making a note or two they had left the scene, promising to do whatever there was to be done.

"It was a storm in a teacup," I said, reassuringly. "Some bloke having a row with his missus. She's been leading him a dance – maybe taunting him about the kid that's on the way, or maybe stopping his tap till the job's over – and he's blown his top and grabbed her."

All of which sounded very reasonable to me, but not to Doreen.

"Trust you to make it the woman's fault," she flared. "Poor Bernadette isn't like that at all. And it wasn't her husband who took her away, it was two great big ugly men – two criminal types. They've murdered her, I know they have. They've dragged her away into the woods and they've raped her and murdered her."

"Now you're being fanciful," I said. "If they were after somebody to rape they wouldn't go for a woman seven or eight months pregnant – not with all those other floosies around. They'd have taken their pick." I leered at her. "They'd have taken you, my darling."

But once again I'd said entirely the wrong thing. In my tin-pot way I'd been paying her a compliment, but I'd used the word 'floosies' in a way that had enabled Doreen to snatch something and hang on.

"I'm not a floosie," she screamed. "How dare you call me that? You men are all the same. Never satisfied unless you're saying insulting things about women. Well I won't have it. I won't have you saying things like that – do you hear me?"

Did I mention that as well as being a very fetching piece of friendly crumpet, Doreen is also a hell-cat when roused? When she fights she does so entirely without fear. No doubt she feels herself bolstered up by the confidence that comes from never having lost a fight? She's never lost one with me, certainly – and that is not because I'm the sort of gentleman who doesn't defend himself against women. Hell, I'd take her on gladly, except that she's too smooth, too guileful, too agile and far too bloody strong. Whenever Doreen comes at me with nails and boots flailing – as she did on this occasion – I adopt my number one tactic that has never been known to let me down. I duck my head, wrap my arms around my face, cross my legs and fall into a foetal crouch – and I hold that position till her temper abates. It never lasts long, thank God! And after it's over she becomes all contrite and wants to make up to me in whichever way she can. We have a favourite way of making up. It's great. And while we were making up I forgot all about Bernadette O'Mahoney and the stupid row she was having with her husband.

✧   ✧   ✧

I was reminded of her again, next morning, when I read the morning paper. Bernadette had been dragged away all right – and so far she hadn't turned up. But the police – whilst concerned about her disappearance on humanitarian grounds – were taking much the same view as I'd taken, that the incident had a background of domestic squabbling. There was a photograph of Bernadette, taken by somebody at the health centre, in which she was posing in her black tights. A single extra leg each side of her, both – I have to say it – more shapely than her own, indicated that the print had been chopped out of a line-up. Well, I still didn't think Bernadette had the sort of magnetism that would drive men wild enough to drag her off and rape her, but I wasn't going to say that to Doreen. I wasn't going to say anything more – ever again – to Doreen on the subject of Mrs. Bernadette O'Mahoney.

I did wonder, briefly, about *Mr.* O'Mahoney. He wasn't mentioned in the article except by oblique reference. They didn't even include his christian name. But the name O'Mahoney would have sounded bells with me if I'd had reason to know the bloke. I'd never heard of him. I consigned him to the scrap heap of my memory, along with his missing pregnant wife.

And very shortly afterwards I had more momentous things to think about. The new topic climbed up on me by degrees. It began when I called in at the Dog and Partridge one evening and stood in the tap-room, chatting with the landlord, Fred Mellish. Now the Dog and Partridge is a place where I sometimes meet Bert Boggis (very secretly, I might say, and always without being seen speaking to one another) but on this occasion I'd written Boggis off as a total loss and I was just in there wetting my whistle. The tap-room was getting fairly crowded. One of the regulars was standing at my elbow, an elderly chap I only know as 'Owd Jimmy' and I was looking straight at Owd Jimmy when he suddenly said, "Hello, Fred."

Nothing much in that, except that he appeared to be looking in the wrong direction. Fred Mellish was standing right in front of me, but Owd Jimmy gave his 'Hello Fred' to somewhere across the room. I wondered if he'd gone blind – or maybe taken up ventriloquism – and I turned to look the way Owd Jimmy was looking.

Striding towards us at the bar, with a great soppy grin spread across his mush, was Fred Head.

Now I have as much control over my facial expressions as most men, but if I'm taken completely by surprise I sometimes lose my grip of the reins. In the ordinary course I wouldn't have spoken to Fred Head beyond the conventional clipped word of greeting, and he certainly wouldn't have wasted much time jawing with me. But as he approached he saw the look on my face – it must have expressed total shock and disbelief – and he joined me with an easy laugh.

"Surprised to see me, Peeper?" he enquired.

"Well, bloody hell, what do you think. I thought you was …"

"So I was. You're quite right there. But they couldn't hold me."

"Couldn't hold you? I don't get it."

Fred Head climbed onto a bar stool and used a pointing finger to order his pint. I paid for it. It was my way of atoning. Fred took off the top couple of inches, then turned back to me.

"I got to be honest, Peeper," he said. "I don't get it either. The buggers seemed so sure. They got me a lie-down to cells, no trouble, and then they kept coming round having a go at me, taunting me, the rotten sods. I told 'em to go and get stuffed, but it didn't do any good. The buggers kept coming. Then this morning, all of a sudden they changed their tune. I was a decent bloke. They dusted me down, gave me my property back, whipped me up in front of court and told the beak it had all been a mistake."

"You were innocent," I said, taking his drift. He looked hard at me and there was a pronounced twinkle in his eye.

"That's right, Peeper. I was innocent. They couldn't prove nothing anyway – and that comes to the same thing."

"How about Cutter and Smithy?" I wondered.

"They're still in, as far as I know," Fred Head said.

SEVEN

And so they were – at that moment – but events were on the change. Fred Head's face was the first I saw fresh from custody, but by no means the last. It was as though, having filmed a sequence showing a number of arrests, the camera had been switched to reverse and the cells were emptying again. I could imagine Boggis getting very crusty about this situation and for some time I revelled in thoughts of his discomfiture. But you can't work with a detective as long and as closely as I have with Albert Boggis without seeing some things from his viewpoint at least some of the time. I started to dislike the series of setbacks, but I still couldn't do a damned thing about it.

Not all the released prisoners were as lucky as Fred Head. Some were merely released on bail pending further enquiries – a sure sign of weakness in the circumstances, I thought – and some were brought before the court and put through preliminary battle stages. Reading the accounts in the papers it soon became obvious that the police had a mixed bag of evidence. In some cases they had enough to secure further remands, but in others they had to throw the towel in. I was glad to see that the evidence against Swanky Alice, Bent Nelson and John Field was strong enough to get them committed for trial to Crown Court, and I was even more pleased, a day or so later, when the same was ordered in respect of Lennie Bethel, Chester Moreland, Big Ginger Fish and Peter David Parrott. I wouldn't have liked any of those bastards to have got clean away.

The case against Cutter Watson and Smithy was a border-liner it seemed, and after a bit of cross-talk in the magistrates' court the police withdrew the charges. This case received more publicity than most of the others, no doubt due to certain pithy remarks made by Mr. Michael Cour-Gandy, the solicitor representing Smithy.

The police have wisely decided not to pursue this matter, he was reported as saying, *and have thus avoided a ringing defeat. For defeat it would certainly have been. The evidence against my client is virtually non-existent and I intend to examine the circumstances of this case very closely, with a view to considering whether to bring a civil action on James Smith's behalf, for unlawful arrest.*

Of course there were conflicting observations from the police inspector in court, the chairman of the bench and the clerk to the magistrates, all of which were gleefully reported, but the outcome was dismally predictable. Smithy and Cutter were released.

And yet it was not the flamboyant Cour-Gandy who made the most widely discussed observations at that trial, but the dull-as-ditchwater Mr. W.L.P. (Potters) Mort, the mouthpiece of Cutter Watson. Mort was as colourful as protoplasm and about as lively. No practising solicitor in the world, I'm sure, has been invited to 'speak up' in court more frequently than Potters Mort has. Yet he managed to say to the police inspector (according to the newspaper account):

"You appear to have lost a bit of evidence, Inspector?"

"I'm instructed not to proceed with the case," the

inspector was reported to have replied. "I am not producing evidence."

"But is it the case that you have something missing?"

"I'm not sure I follow the question, Mr. Mort."

"Well let me put it this way. Has a witness reneged?"

"I'm afraid I'm not in a position to discuss that."

✻   ✻   ✻

But it was a nice theory. I believed it – and so did just about everybody else who had the slightest interest. I went right on believing it, even when Boggis refused to confirm it.

This time I made contact with Boggis without the slightest difficulty, probably because he came chasing after me. I was still a bit cheesed off with him for his obstructive behaviour earlier, and left to my own resources I'd have made him wait many a long day before I got in touch with him again, but a certain summons reached me by a certain route and I couldn't ignore it. We met on a quiet bench in Gresham Park, tucked under some bushes but close enough to the park lake for us to watch the ducks at their pleasures.

"Somebody made a balls of something, Bert?" I asked.

"I'm not here to discuss balls."

Message received and understood. A message which had nothing to do with the purpose of his visit let me say, for that remained a closed book. But sharp and clear I interpreted the signs. Boggis was upset. Things had gone dreadfully wrong. He didn't know who to blame for it, so he blamed himself. He would not be comforted. He had no wish to hear me – or anyone else – clucking sympathy. *But to hell with Bert Boggis.* He wasn't the only one who'd been pissed around in recent times. I'd had my share of tribulation, and Boggis himself had been responsible for most of it.

"If that's your attitude, Bert," I told him, "you might as well up sticks and clear off. You can't blame me this time. It's not my fault that all your chickens have flown the coop."

"Who's talking about chickens?"

"I am, you brainless sod," I said, exasperated. "I don't give a damn what you say. The reason why you've been so bloody untouchable over the past fortnight is because you've been huffing people all over the place and clearing your books. The reason why you're out of sorts today is because somebody found a chink and blew your bloody house down. You're bang in the middle of a losing streak – and that's why you've come to me. So get on with it. I haven't got all day."

"Come to you!" Boggis sneered. "That's the trouble, mate. You think I like slumming? You think I like coming to an unreliable sod like you for help?"

"Charming. Go on, Bert, let's have our own little domestic row. You've succeeded in buggering up everything else, so now have a go at me." I switched on my falsetto voice, something I do from time to time because it annoys Boggis intensely. "I don't love you any more, Albert. I want a divorce. You can have custody of the kids and you can pay me a thousand a week to …"

"Shut your mouth, you ridiculous, witless snot. Can't you see there's people around? What the hell are they going to think?"

"I don't give a damn what they think, old mate. I'm sick of sitting here listening to you say nothing. Every minute counts with me. So – once and for all – are you going to tell me why things have gone wrong and who managed to pull the plug on you?"

"No."

"No?" I stared at Boggis in disbelief. All the cross-talk that had gone on so far was hot air and wasted time, but it wasn't much more than par for the course. We often hedged and messed about like this, but in the end we got down to the meat of the matter, as I'd expected we would this time. His 'No' shook me rigid, because it sounded as though he meant it. "Well if you aren't going to tell me," I finished, "what the hell are we doing sitting here?"

"I want you to do some nosing around," Boggis said, "on a matter that's quite unconnected with recent arrests. It's one off the side of the plate – an awkward little job I've been landed with."

"Go on, then."

"Kidnapping," he said. "Oh it's not your earth-shattering Charles Lindbergh sort of job. More a domestic thing in my view. But the powers that be are riding me, and I need to get something done. I've had men searching all over the shop, but they've come up with nothing so far, so I want you to lend a hand. Sneak around. Talk to people. See what you can find out."

If you've been following the story so far, you'll realize that I didn't need any more information from Boggis, but that was only because I held an ace card he wasn't aware of – and to a lesser extent because I'd read the papers. But I didn't want Bert Boggis to see my hand, so I played it dumb and innocent.

"Oh aye. Well I'll have to know more about it, Bert, starting with the obvious point – who's been kidnapped?"

"A slatterny Irish bitch called Bernadette O'Mahoney," he said.

*   *   *

A likely bloody story, I strongly didn't think.

Not being a recent arrival on these shores fresh from a banana boat, I knew fine well that Boggis was lying in his teeth. The link between all his recent troubles and the kidnapping of Bernadette O'Mahoney was as obvious as the main struts on the Humber Bridge. The fact that Boggis was not prepared to level with me came as no surprise. Indeed. I recognised his attitude as an oft-repeated and very important part of the relationship. Complete frankness on both sides might seem, at first glance, to be the best approach to a partnership such as ours, but in practice that isn't the case. By keeping me in the dark about some things, Boggis was actually protecting me from many pitfalls – and by telling Boggis only as much as I thought he should know, I very often saved him from serious embarrassment. In the present case we had a prime example of a common side-effect of this lack of total open-ness. I knew a little more than Boggis thought I did – and God help me, maybe it was vice versa too.

Anyway, I continued to play stupid and Boggis supplied me with the bare minimum of information about Bernadette. He gave me her address, at the same time explaining that it would be a waste of time going there, because his men were already covering it. She was the wife of Terrence O'Mahoney who lived at the same address. They had no kids – not yet – but the arrival of their first-born was uncomfortably imminent, which (Ha-ha-ha! I thought) was the only reason why Boggis and his bosses were worried about the job. They thought the domestic angle was the likeliest background. Old man O'Mahoney must have some grudge against his wife – maybe she'd been playing away from home or something – and he was prime suspect for the kidnapping, but they'd grilled Terrence O'Mahoney and he'd admitted nothing, hence the need for a few behind the scenes enquiries.

"Any chance of seeing the ransom note?" I wondered.

"What bloody ransom note?"

"Well come along, Bert. Don't tell me there hasn't been one?"

"That's exactly what I do tell you. There hasn't been one."

"In that case – how come you're not chasing a murder? And don't say that never occurred to you, because it must have. Kidnapping is for money – or for something of value at any rate – and if whoever snatched this woman hasn't put in his demand, then it isn't a straight kidnapping. What have you had from these people, Bert?"

"I told you, not a bloody thing."

"And you still say it's a kidnapping?"

"Look, Peeper," (This was his overbearing 'shut-your-mouth-and-listen' attitude, that cut no ice with me.) "I'm just here to say get looking and get listening. I want to know as much as I can about this blasted O'Mahoney woman."

* * *

After we parted I was busy with my thoughts. Try as I might, I couldn't see Bernadette O'Mahoney as the supergrass. Not because there's anything unheard-of about a woman spilling beans, but because Mrs. O'Mahoney couldn't possibly have known enough about big crimes and top class criminals to be able to do it. It had to be her husband, Terrence O'Mahoney, but the trouble there was that I couldn't believe it of him either. Let me remind you that up to then I didn't know Terrence O'Mahoney from the third eunuch from the left in the harem of the Sultan of Beri-bari. I didn't know Bernadette either, apart from having seen her photograph, but that was enough to allow me to dismiss her from the suit. As for O'Mahoney himself, my very ignorance of him bore the seeds of my disbelief. If friend Terrence was a crook – and big, big, big – why had I never heard of him? Conversely, if he wasn't an experienced hard-core villain, how the hell could he be a supergrass? It was all very confusing.

Right from the outset I determined *not* to go for Terrence O'Mahoney. Whether he was or wasn't helping the police made no sort of difference to my own task. Boggis could be relied upon to foster Terrence. He'd asked me to find Bernadette, and that was precisely what I meant to do.

At any rate, I meant to *try* to do it. Where the hell I should start was a problem that caused me considerable headache.

For starters it would be politic to ignore all the likely places on the grounds that Bert Boggis and his merry men would already have done those. He'd as good as said so. If he had men searching for Mrs. O'Mahoney, they were surely looking in the likely places – and if they'd had any joy at all, Boggis would never have come to me. On the other hand, wasn't I taking too much for granted? I had mixed memories of a recent search of the house of Frenchy Watts (or of Peter David Parrott if you like keeping up to date) and part of that memory concerned a warrant. *I also have a warrant to search this house,* the police inspector had said, and he'd been concerned to search for stolen property. Was

Bernadette O'Mahoney considered to be stolen property? Would they require a warrant to search for her? And if they did – did that mean that they'd have to get a separate warrant for every place they searched? Let me digress a moment, at this stage, to make an observation that's become clearer and more important to me as the years have gone by. There's an awful lot of bullshit talked about human rights and police states and abuse of power. If you want me to join in the refrain that goes, *all coppers are bastards*, I'll join in with gusto, but I still won't be able to understand why we tie their hands the way we do. If you're a crook, why shouldn't a copper have a look through your suitcase? If you've got stolen gear in your house, why shouldn't a copper come looking for it – whether you like it or not? And if you're not a crook, but an honest man, why the hell should you object to having a copper ask you questions, search you, look through your house or whatever? I'm very suspicious of those people who won't answer or won't be searched. Some of them are public-spirited people with high-flown ideas about the importance of their own rights – but a lot of them are nothing of the kind.

But enough of that. The plain fact central to the present case was that I – a not very honest hand-rag about town – could do things Boggis couldn't do. Things that Boggis couldn't *officially* do, at any rate. And once I'd reached that conclusion I could see that I needed to begin with the likely places. Frenchy's (Parrott's) house was the obvious place to start, for two reasons. Firstly, having searched it so recently, the police might have given it a miss, and secondly, with Parrott and his crew still in custody, the house would either be empty – or full of Bernadette.

I won't bore you with the saga. I went to the house

and found it in darkness. There was a window loose at
the back and I went inside. Nothing in the attic,
nothing in the cellar and nothing in between. Stevie
Brooks (still languishing in prison) had a big mansion
of a place on the other side of town, but Stevie also had
a wife and a variety of daily helps. I went there and
nosed around. There was no sign of Bernadette
O'Mahoney, or of any activity that might have suggested
she was being held there. I moved on to take a look at
other houses, other places – scores of other houses and
places – and all I succeeded in doing was working
myself to a frazzle. If Bernadette had been lodged
anywhere in town, it was a place I'd never heard of in
connection with the mobs.

I thought all sorts of other things. I wondered if
they'd been crafty enough to take her somewhere well
away, right out of town, maybe as far as the city or
beyond. I wondered if they hadn't taken her anywhere
at all, but had lopped her head off and fed her to a
furnace or dressed her in ready-mix. Well, if she'd
been taken far away, Boggis could go whistle, because I
had no intention of following Bernadette to the ends of
the earth, and if they'd done her in ... *No, they hadn't
done her in*. At least I could be certain of that much.
Because they'd only taken her to bring pressure to bear
on the supergrass and make him retract his evidence.
Anybody with half an intellect could have worked that
out, no bother. The ploy was working very well and
they wanted it to keep on working, so I felt I could
safely discount any suggestion that she might be dead.

No – that wasn't quite right either. I could discount any
risk that they might have intentionally killed her, but I
had still to face the possibility that she might have
upped and died. After all, poor old Bernadette had
been in an interesting condition, and whilst she might

have been quite used to hurling herself around at the health centre, she might have responded less well to having somebody else hurl her around. Heavily pregnant women gave up the ghost sometimes – didn't they? – when subjected to fear and shock. And wouldn't that be a hell of a turn-up for the kidnappers if they found themselves with an unexpected body on their hands?

I spent so much time dwelling on this new theory that I almost convinced myself it must be so – and then I got a grip on my over-imaginative brain and told myself not to be so flaming stupid. Of course they wouldn't shock her or frighten her to that degree. She was their ace card and the game was for very high stakes. They'd wrap Bernadette in cotton wool, cosset her, keep an eye on her condition, fix her up with anything she needed – like pills or potions or sanitary ware or sanitary wear – and almost certainly they'd have a woman in attendance – maybe even a nurse. I'd been going about this job all the wrong way. I should have been thinking of places where they could handle a heavily pregnant woman.

I was at that stage of thinking when I began to work for Doreen.

Putting it that way, it sounds ridiculous but it's almost literally true. Not that Doreen would have paid me – or that I'd ever have taken money from her – but I began to look for Bernadette on Doreen's behalf, simply because she asked me to. I don't think there was ever real friendship between Doreen and Bernadette, but they'd seen each other, week in and week out, at this dreadful sweaty wrestling rink they both frequented, and the abduction of Bernadette had affected Doreen profoundly, strengthening a friendship that might otherwise never have existed.

Days had gone by since the event, and I'd imagined Doreen would have forgotten all about it, but one day, after I'd scoffed my breakfast, she cornered me.

"That poor girl," she said. "They haven't found her yet."

The words, *which girl?*, came to my tongue but I had enough sense not to utter them. I've grown used to Doreen over the years. I can tell when she affords some subject special importance. And if it's important to her, I have a duty to know all about it.

"She'll be all right, kid. They'll find her."

"But that's just the point," she said, a faintly hysterical edge coming to her voice, "they've been looking for her and they can't find her. It's dreadful to think of poor Bernadette being held prisoner in some dirty cellar. We've got to find her."

"You mean we should go rooting around searching for her?"

"Well, why not? If we find her, we can save her."

*   *   *

I now had a new line of enquiry to follow and a new assistant to help me – an assistant who might be expected to supply all those little pointers that women understand and men are ignorant of. In a perfect world we'd have gone straight out, caught a bus, got off at the right stop, knocked on a door and said 'Hello, Bernadette. Come with us. Your troubles are over,' but in my world perfection is as hard to find as Bernadette O'Mahoney was proving to be. We worked together at it for several days – spying on doctors and district nurses, sneaking up on midwives, bobbing into clinics and hospital reception departments and generally playing the sleuth. All to no avail. Am I boring you? Please don't be bored. There's a reason why I had to mention the Doreen slant, even if you won't fully appreciate it till later.

Oddly enough, the minute Doreen got fed up and decided to let me continue alone, I struck oil.

I'd half given up myself. There was a pressing burden of guilt operating on my mind because I hadn't given Stella as much attention as she was used to, and in order to ease that burden I toddled along to the Albion Hotel. Parked alongside the steps at the front entrance was a shiny pram, full of those soft woolly blankets and lace pillows that seem to go with the dirty bums and vomity chops of the very young. Now a pram is a pram in most situations, but outside the Albion Hotel a pram is a source of wonder – and I was wondering like mad. It pleased me to see that the baby had been removed (the rats might have had it if it had been left) but I thought the pram's owner was chancing her arm a bit by leaving her shopping in plastic carrier bags festooned over the pram. Still, it was no business of mine. And what I really wanted to know was who the hell, with a baby, might be calling at the Albion?

Whoever it was, she was calling on Stella. (I say 'she' because it never crossed my mind that it might be a 'he' and I was right.) As soon as I got within reach of the kitchen – Stella's favourite sanctum in which guests are entertained, friends fed and so on – I could hear voices coming through the half open door. This didn't deter me. I shoved the door back and breezed in, exchanging nods with Stella who was busy at the stove.

"Ah, James," she said. "Come and meet an old friend of yours."

The woman who rose from a chair in the corner, her arms full of pink baby, was a picture of blooming motherhood, if a bit on the skinny side. Married life had been good to her and the advent of the offspring even better. I had to stare at her for a minute or two before I realised I knew the face.

"It's Jane Prendergast, isn't it?" I offered.

"Jane Hunker," she said with a tiny frown.

"Hell, yes. I'd forgotten. How is old Bunker these days?"

EIGHT

The culmination was that I got out of the Albion Hotel as quickly as I could, without obliging Stella, and she was far from being chuffed about it – but I'm getting ahead of myself.

The swapping of old helloes with Jane Hunker (Jane Prendergast as was) proceeded for a minute or two, giving me the opportunity of examining Bunker Hunker junior – actual name Gary, as Jane informed me – and congratulating the child on not looking too much like his father. Actually, Gary was rather a pretty child, much more handsome than his father, his mother or any combination of the two, which goes to show that even genes can have kind hearts. I'd met the parents some time earlier – and meeting Jane today was a sure fire reminder of that earlier occasion.(*)

But a little introductory material is necessary here. Jane Prendergast was an ex-resident of the Albion Hotel, having lived there as the common law wife of a man called Matthews. Matthews (who has no part in this story) fell foul of the Frenchy Watts mob, one of whom was a very large and lumpy man called Basil Hunker – fated to be known as Bunker, from B. Hunker, you see – and in the fullness of time, Jane and Bunker made a match. Today I was looking at the

(*) see *GRASS'S FANCY*.

product of that union and being more than pleasantly surprised.

Within minutes of Stella's introduction I was making my excuses and insisting on leaving, in spite of Stella's protestations.

"No need to go, James," she said, sweetly. "Jane will be leaving very soon, won't you Jane?"

"Well, er …"

"You see. So you might as well stay, James, and have a bite."

"Sorry, Stella, I simply can't stay. Something very important has just come to mind and there's no way I can put it off. So cheerio. I'll be by tomorrow. See you then."

And believe me, I hadn't told Stella any lies. Something very important and urgent *had* come up. I had to be outside the Albion, tucked up in some handy corner, when Jane Prendergast came out, so that I could follow her to wherever she was going.

To this day I can't be completely sure why the need to follow Jane impressed itself on me, but it did. It might have been sixth sense, or second sight or some other form of intuition, but a curious coming together of facts helped it along. For several days past, I'd been looking for a pregnant woman who was likely to become a mother at any time, I'd been seeing her as having to be attended by another women who would have to be on the side of the ungodly, I'd toured all sorts of centres of medicine in search of a lead and I'd kept in my mind, all this time, the fact that whatever and wherever the set-up was, it would have to be connected with one or other of the leading mobs in town. Moreover, my enquiries had been pretty exhaustive and I'd begun to run out of new possibilities, so when the Jane Prendergast angle offered itself I was ready to snatch at anything.

Jane was a mother and therefore experienced in the needs of pregnant women. She was bent as a corkscrew – a shoplifter mainly, but with at least one conviction for robbery – and she was married to Basil Hunker, who until a year or so ago had been one of Frenchy Watt's right hand men. Not much to go on, you might think, but there was one further item I could add – an item small in itself, but waxing larger when added to the rest. Jane's shopping, festooned around her pram in plastic bags. I've got the sort of memory that records things without taking much notice. I'd seen those bags on the way in, and now I checked them on the way out. There were four, and three of them bore the same name.

BOOTS – THE CHEMISTS.

If I give you a sneak preview by saying that my suspicions proved well-founded, that's only to prevent you wondering what sort of fool would follow up a lead as slender as that. It was slender all right – and looked at in retrospect it was fit only to be ignored – but I was struggling for something to do, so I followed her.

The house she led me to was quite a small one, semi-detached, not at all the kind of house where I'd expect a kidnapped woman to be lodged. So I was put off at the outset, but then I started to see things more favourably. The first thing I saw was a big blue Transit van parked in the drive. The place I'd chosen for spying was too far away for me to read the van's registration number, but judging from its immaculate condition it was a recent model. Where, I wondered, had Bunker found the money for a van like that?

And then I saw Bunker himself. He came from the rear of the house and walked up the side path. There were two other men with him, both strangers to me. They were strong looking, well made men, but if you'd cast the two of them in one mould they wouldn't have made a single Bunker, who was built like a brick shithouse. One of the men climbed into the van and backed it out of the drive. I expected to see him drive away, instead of which he three-point turned the van and reversed back into the drive. Bunker and the second stranger opened the back doors of the van and took out a number of packages neatly wrapped in brown paper. They carried them into the house by the front door, which opened as they reached the doorstep, for all the world like one of those supermarket doors controlled by an electronic ray. The man who had driven the van now closed the back doors and followed the others into the house. I waited for one or all of them to come out again, but nobody came out.

After a while I set out to explore. I found that by taking a narrow footpath further along the street I could walk round to the back of the house. A number of surprises lay in store for me. The first was the discovery that these houses had abnormally large back gardens – and Bunker's plainly the largest of all. Moreover, all the fronts of the houses had been very skimpily fenced, and the next surprise came when I realised that this was not so at the rear. Thick yew and privet hedges were the order of the day. I was surprised to see the top of a washing-line pole in one garden – surprised because it must have been twenty feet tall, or I'd never have seen it over the boundary hedge. But the greatest surprise of all came when I had climbed a gate into the grounds at the back of Bunker's house and threaded my way through a jungle of shrubs until the house came in sight. In the small clearing right behind the house – a bare patch in a jungle – two women were taking a stroll. One was Jane Prendergast. The other was a lady I'd only ever seen a photograph of before, but even if she hadn't been pregnant, which she largely and plainly was, I'd still have recognised Bernadette O'Mahoney.

I curbed the rush of impetuosity which was urging me to dash from cover, grab Bernadette, repulse any counter attack from Jane Prendergast (remember, her married name is Hunker) and bear the captive to safety. For one thing, I doubted my ability to do it. The O'Mahoney woman was a hell of a lump to drag around, I knew Jane Prendergast wouldn't sit and sulk while I made my getaway and it only required a couple of screams from her to bring Bunker and his mates hot-footing to save the day. Besides, too many people would recognise me. Jane would certainly see me, even if Bunker didn't, and the word would go round that I was the prime mover behind the redemption of Bernadette O'Mahoney. That would certainly never do. I had to have clean hands. A hint of suspicion could ruin my whole career.

So I crouched there among the bushes and watched Bernadette taking her exercise. It occurred to me that her captors hadn't taken very strict precautions to ensure she didn't escape. I'd have expected at least one man to be with her all the time in addition to her present chaperon, so that any attempt at releasing her – or any attempt at escape for that matter – could be put down. I even wondered why they allowed her to walk free, when bastards like Bunker Hunker might have been expected to tie her hands, gag her, or whatever.

The attendant circumstances, I supposed, were enough to supply the answers. For all the gang knew, nobody else could be aware of the whereabouts of Bernadette, so an opposition attack was unlikely. The back garden was a remarkably private place – much more private than could ever be suspected by someone seeing only the front of the house – and to Bernadette the confines of her exercise yard probably seemed impenetrable. There were neighbours, one had to presume, but so much foliage had been allowed to grow between Bunker's back garden and those adjoining that the neighbours would be unlikely to see or hear anything. Bernadette herself seemed to be taking her captivity with no great concern. She was chatting with Jane Prendergast, and although neither woman was smiling they didn't give the appearance of being particularly unfriendly. Bernadette would have been given the gypsy's warning, I supposed – something along the lines of, *one false move and we'll drop the gate on you* – and she'd feel her position to be so hopeless that there was no alternative but to play along.

Unless ...? I allowed myself one unchivalrous thought – namely that Bernadette herself was in some way party to the proceedings – but I didn't allow it to linger. I had Doreen's description of her kidnapping – she had resisted fiercely, both physically and vocally – and that hadn't sounded like somebody going of her own free will. Still, it was better to look at the thing from all angles. I looked at it from this new angle – and dismissed the thought.

My next step was to devise a plan for rescue. It seemed pretty obvious that this exercise break – more than likely a daily event – was the time to strike, for then there was only the Prendergast bird to contend with. On the other hand, if I couldn't do it this time, how the hell could I do it next time, unless I brought reinforcements? It occurred to me then – as I'm sure it must have occurred to you – that my best plan would have been to retire, telephone Bert Boggis and give him the address. Bert would have brought enough men to take the place apart brick by brick. But I had no intention of pandering to Boggis if I could help it. There was money in Bernadette – not ransom money, but reward money – and I meant to stake a sole claim to it. Come what may, this had to be an individual job. But I had to have help, and offhand the only person I could think of who would help me without asking too many questions, was Doreen.

Thinking on this, I realised that Doreen's help was going to be very necessary in another way. Doreen knew Bernadette – and more importantly, Bernadette knew Doreen. Bernadette had never seen me before. I'm not bad looking once you get to know me, but at first meeting I'm said to look a bit of a horror. So what reaction could I expect from Bernadette if I suddenly burst out of the trees, grabbed her and began to back away? She'd raise the roof of course. She'd scream and swear and kick out – and I'd never get her anywhere near the back gate. Hell, no. There was no way I could rescue Bernadette without priming her first. And I couldn't even prime her, because she didn't know me. Doreen would have to do the priming.

I was warming to the task now. I could see the importance of cutting Bernadette in on my plan – and I realised also that it would have to be done in advance. It would be no use Doreen running up to her and trying to explain the position under Jane Prendergast's nose. But what, if any, was the alternative? Would there ever be a time and a place when Bernadette

O'Mahoney was on her own?

I tried to climb into the mind of my old mate Bunker Hunker with a view to working out how he'd organise his sentries. There'd be a rota of some sort, with Bunker taking his stint in turn, and between them they'd keep watch on their prisoner night and day. The only times when they might relax vigilance would be when she had to take a bath, go to the loo or crash her head to sleep. It was possible that they'd even have her watched then, by having Jane Prendergast go with her to the bog and sleep in the same bedroom with her, but somehow I didn't think so. In relation to the bathroom and the bog it didn't matter a damn anyway, since there was no chance of getting to her in either of those situations, but her bedroom might offer a slight chance.

I'd already half-decided which was Bernadette's bedroom, and now – because eventually you have to reach a decision – I went firm on it. There was a low roof at the rear of the house – a sun-lounge roof – and over it, three separate bedroom windows. It was more than coincidence, I thought, that the middle window had its curtains shut. They were keeping out unwanted viewers. That had to be her room. The low roof offered a good access route to the window and, for the moment at least, one of the transoms was ajar.

How would Bunker guard that room? There might well be a lock on the door – but whether there was a lock or not, there'd be a sentry on the landing. I felt pretty sure, though, that they wouldn't post a sentry outside, at the rear. If they did, it was curtains, but I had to gamble that they wouldn't. And if they didn't, it was possible. Risky, but possible.

So I made my plans to fit the case. There would be no passing of notes – for there was too much risk of a note passing into the wrong hands – but I'd arrange it so that Bernadette and Doreen could have a proper, face to face discussion at the most opportune time.

＊   ＊   ＊

The most opportune time, in my view, was the wee small hours, when all the players except the night sentry would be fast asleep. There was a fifty fifty chance that the sentry might be sleeping too, at that hour, especially if it happened to be Bunker's turn. It wasn't Doreen's idea of the best time for anything, but she's a good girl and at 2-30 a.m. next day she was standing beside me between the bushes in Bunker's back garden. She was doing a lot of yawning, but there was excitement in her to. I could see her eyes sparkling in the light of the moon.

The back of the house was in darkness, but on the way in I'd checked the front, and I knew there was a night light glowing. I cast a keen eye over the approach route. My long experience as a burglar was helping me now. The fence on the right was as good as a ladder to the garage roof, the crossing from garage to sun-lounge roof was less than a stride and the way was open to Bernadette's room. But the bloody window wasn't open. I can't say I was surprised about that, but I was disappointed. It meant a change in my plans. I'd hoped to send Doreen on her own, but now I'd have to go with her.

"Now listen," I said in a final briefing. "We can manage without heroics. Waken the wrong people and we'll be in deep trouble. So off you go. I'm right behind you. Keep your eyes and ears open and be ready to run like hell if anything goes wrong."

I took one last despairing look at her mini skirt, but

I didn't return to the argument we'd had about it. As a mere male, with all a male's hang-ups, I'd suggested she should wear trousers because there was climbing to be done, but Doreen had assured me she felt more free in her skirt, and even if she did display her knickers it wouldn't matter a damn, because there'd be nobody there to see at that ungodly hour. Following her up the struts of the fence with my head almost bumping against her tight little bum, I made a mental note to tell her how mistaken she had been.

We sneaked across the sun-lounge roof like a couple of elopers. I was carrying a small torch – and a number of other essentials. Peeping in through a chink in the curtains I could see a bar of yellow light glowing in the crack under the bedroom door but the room was in complete darkness. I shoved an ear to the glass and listened. Somebody was snoring fit to explode. It was that loud, rumbling stuff with no clear edges and I almost convinced myself I could hear more than one sleeper.

"I'm going to chance it," I told Doreen. "So get over by the fence and be ready to take off."

But after I'd risked a first flash of the torch I beckoned her back and her face joined mine, peering along the beam of the torch. The room was quite small. There was a chair, a bed and a narrow wardrobe, but nothing else. It was a single bed and there was a single occupant. I could see her face in the glow of the torch and I could also see a mound running almost the length of the bed that looked like a relief map of Ben Nevis. I didn't really need Doreen's confirmation, but I thought I'd have it to be on the safe side.

"Is that her?" I whispered.

"That's her all right." She chuckled. "Poor

Bernadette."

"Poor Bernadette be buggered. It'll be poor us if we make too much noise. So for Christ's sake waken her gently. Whisper in her ear or something and shove your hand over her mouth if she starts screaming. Come on, kid. Look sharp." I said, as she hesitated.

"How can I, you great berk? The windows are fastened."

"Give me a minute," I said, brandishing a certain implement of my own design. "I'm a pretty dab hand at windows."

✳   ✳   ✳

I opened a transom first, then reached inside, unhooked a casement and opened it wide. Casement windows are just like small doors. Doreen has no experience as a burglar (as far as I know) but she cocked a leg over the sill and was inside in half a second. I left the window standing wide (you never know when you have to take a last minute flying header) then retired to the edge of the roof, where I sat with my legs dangling. The job was as good as done. Any minute now we'd be on our way. It wouldn't take Doreen long to pass on the instructions I'd drummed into her.

I looked out across the silent, moonlit garden. That was where it would all start to happen. They'd have a hell of a shock coming tomorrow, Bunker and his mates. I'd have a car waiting in the alley at the back (I'd have to pinch one – I've never been able to afford one of my own) and it would just be a matter of jollying Bernadette across the clearing and down the length of the shrubbery. By the time Doreen had briefed her, Bernadette would know exactly what to do.

Keep close to the Prendergast bitch, my instructions directed. *Try to get her to walk you away from the house, over towards the shrubbery. I'll pick the best time. When you hear me whistle, give Jane Prendergast a hefty shove and nip into the bushes. We'll be right there, waiting to spirit you away.*

There was silence from the house – a heartening sign. I waited a while, feeling the time dragging like mad. I was starting to get worried when Doreen's leg appeared through the window, followed by her backside and the rest of her. She stood there for a minute, looking back into the room.

"Close the window," I hissed, "and get yourself over here."

Doreen didn't seem to have heard me. I took a step in her direction, meaning to hurry her along.

And then the disturbance that made my heart leap and stop.

There was a great sound of puffing and creaking and vastness filled the window frame. It was Bunker Hunker. He'd caught us at it, and now he'd grab Doreen. Bunker could never have caught me, but I'd have to surrender anyway, since I could never leave her in the hands of a bastard like that. I saw the meaty arm come out and make a wild grab at Doreen and I knew it was all over.

But it wasn't Bunker – it was Bernadette.

"What the hell's happening?" I snapped.

Doreen flashed me a cheeky grin and her voice was filled with half-suppressed glee.

"I told her, but it was no good. She won't wait till tomorrow."

I looked at the tangle of fence-post legs, fat buttocks and proud belly protruding from the window like some mammoth-pup on its way into the world. I scowled at Doreen.

"Christ, woman. She's in no state to go climbing off roofs."

"Chauvinist," she said, grinning more widely. "They do a good job at the health centre. Bernadette's a damned sight fitter than you are."

NINE

And let me say, it was no lie. Give the woman credit, she nipped down off that roof like an emigrating squirrel and when she strode over to join Doreen and me on the lawn I didn't hear a single pant. We melted away into the bushes where we paused to re-group.

"It's a hell of a long walk home," I told them, "and some of us aren't as fit as we used to be. So you two hang about here while I go and rustle up some transport. I'll go the front way."

The Transit van was still parked in the driveway. I had a good look round to make sure nobody was watching, then I nipped up to the driver's door and peeped in. The keys dangled in the lock. It's a funny thing, but professional thieves are often more careless than ordinary people, especially on their own middens. By the look of things it had never occurred to Bunker and his mates that some light fingered sod might nick the van.

Or then again, maybe it had. Starting the van would be no problem, but unless I could devise a ramp there was no way I could drive it away. I'd been too busy to notice until now, but parked in front of it was another van, a titchy little thing, a Morris Mini in a sort of dirty cream colour. Bunker's car, perhaps? Always assuming a bloke like Bunker could squeeze into it.

Which gave rise to the question, could Bernadette

squeeze into it? I shifted my attention to the Mini – it had four wheels and an engine, and I'm not a proud man – and would you believe it, no keys. I tried the driver's door – it was unlocked. So, I found, was the passenger door. There wouldn't be room for three on the front seats but the back was open, so at a pinch Doreen could ride in there. I tried to conjure up a mental picture of Bernadette, then slotted the shape into the passenger door. It would just about fit, if we heaved a little. It would have to fit – or we'd need to look elsewhere.

I'd just about committed myself to using the Mini when one of those seemingly unprompted re-thinks crept up on me. Wasn't I giving in too easily? Did I really have to settle for a clapped out Mini, maybe twenty years old, when I could ride off in style in a nearly brand new Transit van? Not if I knew anything about motor cars.

Reaching into the Mini, I twiddled the gear stick into neutral. Then I released the handbrake. I tried the steering – it moved easily. There probably hadn't been a steering lock on this old model, but if there had, it wasn't working any more. I climbed out and checked the alignment of the front wheels. They were skewed a bit to the left. I ducked inside again, made an adjustment, checked again. The little van would run straight ahead now, if the wheels held track.

But I'd have to get my timing absolutely right. I sneaked back to round up the girls, steered them up the side path and helped them into the Transit van. The door creaked a bit, and the noise seemed to blast through the stillness, but apart from the little night light I had noticed earlier, Bunker's house remained in darkness. I climbed in and eased the door shut after me. We were as good as away.

I twisted the key and the engine coughed, so I twisted it again and the engine coughed again. I fiddled in the dark to see if there was a choke I should be pulling – and all at once it wasn't dark any more. Behind me, Bunker's house was lit up like one of Harrods' showcases. I had another twist at the key and got half a spark, but once again it died on me.

Meanwhile things were happening at the house. Casting a fearful eye that way, I saw the front door open and a man dressed in long john underwear stuck his leg out. He seemed scared to advance further and I gave the ignition a couple of quick twists, hoping I might still get away before he plucked the guts up to brave the cold. I kept on twisting and watching. The man in long johns suddenly shot forward, to measure his length on the front lawn, and behind him was a terribly enraged Bunker. In what they usually call a fleeting glance I saw that great mountain of white flesh and realised that he was starkers. I could see the biggest thing about him – the thing that I supposed had attracted Jane Prendergast in the first place – and I hoped Doreen wasn't seeing it too – or she'd never be satisfied with me again.

But it was Bunker's other weapon that really alarmed me. I couldn't tell at the distance what make or type it was, but it was a pistol of some sort. He was waving it about and shouting angrily. I knew it was only a matter of seconds before he started blasting off.

I remember wondering what the hell I was going to do. If I'd been alone the question would never have arisen, for I'd have been away by now, doing a shade over fifty along the street. But there was no way the girls could run. Doreen might have – she'd most likely have given it a try if it hadn't been for Bernadette, but Bernadette hadn't enough time even to struggle out of the van. So the only thing I could do was throw my hands in the air and plead with Bunker not to shoot. I was ready to do that. I had a last twist at the ignition key. The bloody thing fired.

And so did Bunker, but quite honestly I didn't give a damn any more. I saw the flash out of the corner of my eye and I heard the slug smack into the side of the van, but I was moving now, and no Bunker, gun or clapped out Mini was going to stop me.

The Transit collided quite gently with the Mini and propelled it through the front gate into the street. As I increased sped and put on a right hand lock the two vehicles parted company. The instant I cleared the Mini I revved like mad out of sheer exuberance, then threw a higher gear and went burning away from that house as though the hounds of hell were after me.

My eyes glued to the mirror, I was amazed to see Bunker, still naked as a baby, come running out of his path and shoot across the street towards the stranded Mini. I chuckled because I was bubbling with confidence. Whatever happened, Bunker would be at a distinct disadvantage without his clothes – and it had been bad enough trying to start the Transit. With the Mini, he had no chance.

The Mini started first time – sweet as a nut. Before I swung round the first corner I knew the Mini was right on my tail.

* * *

Whenever I hear people say how wonderful our policemen are, my mind goes back to the escape from bare Bunker and I'm forced to agree with the sentiment. But a number of things happened before the ordeal was over. The Transit had maybe three

hundred yards start on the Mini and for a while I tried
to consolidate. But give Bunker Hunker every credit,
he can make a Mini move. On top of that, he could
corner better than I could, and gradually he began to
whittle down the distance between us till I could almost
feel his breath on the back of my neck. The girls were
terrified. I don't like to be hard on women, and I
acknowledge that they have a hell of a lot going for
them, but there's something about a car chase that
knocks them right out. I was a bit scared myself. Not
only was Bunker bigger than me but he also had a gun.
At least I presumed he still had it. The gun was bad
enough, but one other thing exercised my mind. If it
came to a showdown, Bunker would blow the gaff on
me. I've often said how much I dislike the name
'Peeper' but when it comes right down to hey-lads-hey,
I'd much rather have it than 'Mud'.

He hadn't seen my face yet, and that was the way I
meant to have things stay. "Sit tight and hang on,
girls," I told them in an effort to give them confidence.
"I'll shake this bastard off our tail before I'm
through."

There was a big chunk of waste ground covered with
cinders, building rubble and piles of discarded garbage
that ran behind a factory on the edge of town. I headed
for it, convinced that the Transit would sail over it
without any trouble but the Mini would ground and
die. Not a bit of it. I picked the worst route I could
find, but Bunker lost no more than a few yards. I came
to a wooden fence bordering a country lane, crashed
through the fence sending bits of plank flying all over
the place. The Mini followed me through the gap and
emerged unscathed. In my moment of deep despair I
recognised the lane and had a sudden inspiration. Just
ahead of me there was a ford – a hollow in the road

where a stream crossed and where vehicles could only proceed with care. But the Transit had plenty of clearance – and the Mini hadn't. I hit the ford at speed, sending spray in every direction, and the waters closed again to engulf the Mini. The joy I felt as I glanced in my mirror dissolved into dust and ashes. The Mini was through and still running.

The police car was lying in wait for us on one of the main approaches to town. I'd stolen a yard or two on the Mini and as I breasted the brow of a hill I saw the police car parked up alongside the nearside pavement. The Transit offered a good angle of view and I had time to hit the brakes, firmly but smoothly, so that by the time I reached the police car I was moving quite sedately.

Not so Bunker.

Crouched low down in his little van, Bunker never saw the police car until he was right on top of it – and by that time he was moving like the clappers of hell. He made no attempt to slow down – knowing damned well it was much too late for that – and he passed the police car in a blur. I saw the Mini shudder as it drew level with the slowly moving Transit and Bunker fought against his deep desire to stop and grapple with us. But already the blue light was flashing and that awful two-tone horn ringing in the night air. The Mini went away from us like a rocket with the coppers burning their blue flames in his wake – and both disappeared from sight.

*   *   *

We lodged Bernadette O'Mahoney in the spare room at Doreen's house – and if that sounds a simple operation, don't be misled.

In the first place, the last place on earth Bernadette

wanted to be lodged was the spare room at Doreen's house. They put up no quarrel for maybe ten minutes – they were both too busy calming themselves down and soaking their shattered nerves in cups of hot tea – but once the sweating had stopped I found myself facing attack on both flanks. Bernadette wanted to go home, to be amongst her own trinkets in familiar surroundings, and if she couldn't go home she wanted to be taken to wherever her husband happened to be. I thought I knew where I could find Terrence O'Mahoney, but I wasn't going anywhere near the nick if I could help it. And funnily enough, the nick was exactly where Doreen wanted me to go. An incurable believer in a well ordered society, Doreen had the bee in her bonnet that we ought to hand over the problem – and Bernadette – to the police. It took a lot of talking to convince them we should play it my way.

"Look," I said, when I realised they were both ganging up on me. "This chasing about to find Bernadette is really no business of mine. I've taken a lot of chances tonight, trying to help you two out, and I'm not going to have you drop me in the cart. We have to play this thing very cagey for a couple of days. We have to lie low."

"Why?" Doreen questioned.

"Why?" Bernadette wanted to know.

So I explained the case as follows. Some of the stuff I told them was true, some I had to adjust slightly, to cover my own tracks and the rest was downright bloody lies. Maybe I ought have been ashamed, but Hell's teeth! You've simply got to be firm with women if you want to keep a yard or two ahead of them.

"That gang of roughs who kidnapped Bernadette, they're a mean lot. I don't know why I'm telling you that, after what happened a few minutes ago. But I

know the boss – the big bloke called Bunker Hunker –
and he's very bad news. Bunker won't be pleased with
either of you – and he certainly won't be pleased with
me, because he'll blame me for having organised it all.
The fact is, he'll be mad as a gamecock and if he gets
his hands on us, we're finished. So he'll be looking for
us – and one of the first places he'll look is your home,
Bernadette. I'm willing to bet he's got men there now,
hanging about in the shadows, waiting to see if you're
daft enough to go there. He'll have other men at the
nick – not right there in the building, because not even
Bunker would have that much nerve, but somewhere in
the vicinity, watching the approaches – so the minute
we take you anywhere near the police station, the job's
blown. He may not be able to grab you, *but he'll know
who we are*.

"That's our strongest card at the moment – the fact
that he doesn't know who it was that came to his house,
nipped in and got you out. He doesn't know Doreen at
all. He knows me, but so far he doesn't know I'm tied
up in it. So he can't come looking for us."

"They might come looking for the van," Doreen
said.

Jesus wept! The van.

I'd forgotten all about the van. My mind had been
full of the problems of Bernadette, and in the heat of
the time I'd been so relieved to shake Bunker off my
tail that I'd simply drawn up in the front of Doreen's
house, climbed out and left the damned van there. The
knell of doom was ringing in my ears. It must be half
an hour since we'd kicked the hornets' nest over at
Bunker's house, fifteen minutes at the very least since
I'd shaken Bunker off. Plenty of time there to regroup,
in fact it was a miracle they weren't here already,
thumping on the door and howling their lust for

blood. I was being naive again – surely to God they *were* here already, crouched beside the van, waiting for me to show my face.

I crept out of the front door on hands and knees, my eyes busy for the flash of gunshots. They say you don't duck the one with your name on it, but I was going to have a damned good try. Nothing happened. The van was still there and the street was deserted. *The crafty buggers must be hiding in the van, waiting for me to board.* I slid across the pavement, rose and peeped in. The van was empty. Well, it was muck or nettles now. I leaped aboard, gunned the engine and shot away down the street. I drove maybe a mile and a half along a ziz-zag route, finishing up three quarters of a mile from home. I stuck the van up a back street, tucked in between a builder's skip and the chestnut fencing round a bowling green. Then I set off to walk home.

It had been a mighty close run thing.

Several times during my journey home I had to slip into doorways when cars went hammering by. Ordinary cars on ordinary journeys? I didn't think so for a minute – not those cars, going at that speed and at such an unearthly hour. The hunt was on – and the fox had only a short start on the hounds. I was close to my home, walking along the very next street, when a yellow Mini passed me, going like a bullet. The bloke at the wheel had clothes on – and he wasn't Bunker – but I was very relieved he didn't see me, because it might have been the same Mini.

*   *   *

But with the Transit van out of the way I felt a good deal easier – and in some ways the situation at home had also eased. The few seeds I'd sown before setting off to ditch the van had begun to germinate. Doreen and Bernadette were as thick as thieves, chatting and chuckling over a breakfast that was too early by any standards, and I was able to go on with my task of persuading them to stay put. I explained to them how we were criminals ourselves. Not only had we pinched a van, we'd also committed burglary by breaking into Bunker's house – and even though I'd been the one to commit those offences, the two girls would be considered accomplices. (I told you a lot of this was lies, but what the hell?) I went on to explain that we couldn't go to the police anyway, because the minute they saw Bernadette they'd arrest Doreen and me for kidnapping. This didn't get by without eliciting some little protest.

"Rubbish," Doreen said. "Bernadette would just have to tell them her story and after that we'd be heroes."

"Oh yeah?" I defended, "and suppose they didn't believe her, what then? There's such things as brainwashing, you know. They'd say we'd worked on Bernadette till she didn't know what she was saying. The police can be damned hard people to convince, sometimes."

Convincing Bernadette and Doreen was no mean task either, but I managed it after a while. But there were rumblings of discontent.

"She can't stop here for ever," Doreen insisted.

"I can't stop here for ever," Bernadette pointed out. "I want to go home to Terrence. And I've got the baby to think about. Any minute now it'll be the ante-natal clinic for me. It's all right telling me I've got to hide, but I can't hide and go to the ante-natal clinic as well. Besides, suppose I'm taken ill? You'd have to get a doctor then – and if a doctor came and found me here you'd be in even worse trouble."

"So what happens now?" Doreen wanted to know. "Sooner or later we've got to tell the police. I say we should do it straight away."

"No. Leave it to me, Doreen. Let me pave the way first."

"How can you pave the way? Who's going to believe you?"

"That man who arrested me last time I was in. The one who put in a good word for me. What was his name? Boggis. That's it."

"You mean you'll go and talk to him?"

I said I would, and they believed me. And once I'd done that, I began to work on Bernadette. I knew she could help me crack the case. I started off nice and easy, trying to settle her down.

"How did they treat you at that place?" I grinned at her blank stare. "What I mean is, did they try any rough stuff at all?"

"Rough stuff? No, not really. Except at the start. There was just a little bit to begin with, but it was my own fault, I suppose."

"Your own fault? How can that be? And when was the start?"

"Well, when they rushed me out of the health centre. I didn't want to go. And then when they put me in the van, I was shouting a bit and struggling. They held me down and put a cloth over my mouth. When I stopped shouting they left me alone." She paused. "Except that …"

"Except that what?"

"Except for the first night. I tried to get away, you see. They let me out in the back garden with that Jane woman and I ran up the path to the street. The big man caught me – the Bunker man – and he slapped me across the face. I knew it was no good trying to run again, so I didn't bother – and after that they left me alone."

"What were they supposed to be doing with you?"

"How do you mean?"

"Well, why did they take you? Did they tell you anything?"

"No – not really."

She was lying and I could tell at a glance. I was bursting to know why she was lying but I knew it would do no good to spark off a shouting match, so I went on playing it nice and easy.

"Surely they must have mentioned something? A ransom, maybe?"

"No. They never said anything about a ransom."

"That strikes me as very curious, Bernadette. These people are crooks. They don't do anything unless there's a bob or two to be had from it. If there was no ransom, what did they hope to gain?"

"I honestly don't know."

But she dishonestly did know – and the evidence of her attempt to mislead me was plain on her face. I could have accused her, if I'd thought it might help, but I didn't think it would. And yet I was all through playing around with her. I knew a better way of putting her on the spot.

"Tell me about Terrence O'Mahoney," I invited.

"My husband? What about him?"

"I don't know, girl. I want you to tell me."

"Tell you what? What do you want to know about him?"

"I'm not sure, but let's start at the beginning. Give me date and place of birth, full name, description, that sort of thing."

"What the hell would you want to know that for?"

"What about criminal convictions? Present whereabouts?"

"I've had enough of this. I didn't come here to discuss Terrence. I shouldn't have come here in the first place. Give me one good reason why I should tell you anything about Terrence."

"All right then. Because you told Bunker Hunker. He asked you about Terrence, didn't he? You told him, now you can tell me."

And after a bit more weaving to and fro, she did. But you don't want chapter and verse of my conversation with Bernadette O'Mahoney. All you want to know is the general outcome, so let me give you a quick summary of it.

Terrence and Bernadette O'Mahoney were both natives of Omagh, in Northern Ireland, and they had lived there all their lives until just over a year earlier. Terrence had crossed the sea, alone, on the promise of a job. She didn't know what the job was, but it seemed to bring in a fair bit of money, and after a month or two he'd been able to put a deposit on a house and bring Bernadette over to live with him. That was about eight or nine months ago (hence her present interesting condition) and since then he'd continued to work at his job, wherever and whatever it was.

Throughout our chat, Bernadette insisted that Terrence had never been connected with the I.R.A. but I wasn't at all sure I believed her. He had convictions for theft and screwing (burglary I mean, not copulation) and also for offences involving explosives, but all his convictions were in Ireland. It was possible that Terrence would shortly break his duck in England, though. She wasn't exactly sure where he'd got to, but she thought he was in a cell down at the police station. She didn't know what the charge was, if any. The police had brought him home – a few days before the day when Bernadette was kidnapped – and after searching the house they'd taken Terrence away again. Had they taken anything away from the house – anything that might explain what they were holding him for? Bernadette didn't think so.

Having started talking, she was ready to say a bit more about Bunker and his mob. Bunker had certainly shown an interest in Terrence O'Mahoney, but he hadn't made it clear what his interest was. She wasn't sure whether he'd actually said it or not, but Bunker had at least given her the impression that they were using her in some way to bring pressure on her husband.

She couldn't tell me any more, or so she said. I had mixed feelings about Bernadette, I must admit. I didn't think she was working against us, but I got the impression she was holding something back in her own interests. It didn't matter a great deal. I let her keep her secrets.

The girls were both tired so I packed them off to bed. I've got to admit, I was tired too, but there was no way I could go to sleep with so much weighing on my mind. So I brewed up yet again, then sat in a chair and dozed till the morning paper came.

There was nothing about Bernadette. Well, I didn't imagine Bunker would wish to publicize his loss, but in any case those events had happened too recently to catch the morning paper. The same applied to cases involving naked men driving Mini vans, so I didn't bother looking. But there was one item that caught my eye and I read it with a great deal of interest.

In connection with a long list of recent offences of robbery and burglary, the police had come into possession of a large amount of property, jewellery, crockery, fancy goods, cameras and a host of other goodies, some of which had not been identified by their owners. In the hope of establishing ownership of these items, the police had organised a display, which was being held at the Town Police Headquarters during the next few days. People who had lost property – or thought they might be able to help with identification – were asked to attend at the police station and cast an eye over the display.

I wondered how this tied in with Swanky Alice and Peter David Parrott and Fred Head and Bunker Hunker and all the rest, with special reference to Terrence O'Mahoney – and the answer I gave myself was, *one hell of a lot.*

I checked my watch. It was coming up nine o'clock in the morning. I set off in search of Bert Boggis.

TEN

My breast was filled with a spirit of bravado. No skulking about in telephone booths for me. No whispered messages passed through intermediaries, followed by clandestine confabs in quiet corners. Today I marched straight up to the nick, in at the front door, over to the public counter. There's a bell on the counter to summon the duty public-servant-constable. I hammered on it and stood there waiting, bold as brass. He came, looking suitably subservient.

"Yes, sir. Can I help you?"

"Which way to the exhibition?" I asked grandly.

"The exhibition, sir?"

"That's right, the exhibition. You've got a lot of loot on show, haven't you? You must have. It's in the papers."

"Oh, that. You've had your house burgled, have you, sir?"

"As it happens, no I haven't. I didn't know you had to have your house screwed first. The bit I read in the papers said that …"

"Oh no, sir. That's not necessary. Anybody can have a look round if they think they can help. Your name and address, sir?"

Hell, I hadn't counted on this. I'd expected to follow the crowd through to the display room and stand there with nobody taking a blind bit of notice. If I'd thought they'd want to know who I was, I'd have gone back to my hole-in-the-corner meetings. But it was too late to grumble now. I grinned disarmingly and gave the details.

"Thank you, sir," he said, scribbling them down. "And now if you'll step this way I'll show you through to the property room."

I followed the bloke, feeling pretty proud of myself. I'd never been called 'sir' so many times in my life before and I must admit it went down rather well. But I forgot about that little thrill half a minute later, when he ushered me into the presence of a lot of other things I'd never seen so many of before.

"If you see anything you recognise, sir," the constable said, "all you have to do is point it out to one of the duty officers and tell him what you know. He'll take it down in a statement."

So much for my expectation of a crowd. There were three other people in the room, one in uniform and two in plain clothes, but I could tell by the all-embracing gesture my guide had given that all three were bobbies. In a very real way, their presence – and the absence of other people to mingle with – put paid to the plan I'd originally had in mind. I'm familiar with the lay-out at the nick, you see, and I can find the back way to the private office of Detective Sergeant Albert Boggis without much difficult. I'd intended to mingle with the crowd till I could nip through to the back corridor and along to meet Bert. It was impossible now, with three sets of beady eyes centred on a single little me.

But the vast array of splendid items spread before me on long trestle tables more than made up for any disappointment I might have felt. There were wrist-watches, fob-watches, lapel-watches, gold hunters; large clocks, small clocks, metal clocks, wooden clocks, plain clocks, jewelled clocks, grandfather clocks and travelling alarms; bracelets, bangles, necklaces, pendants, rings, ear-rings, brooches, lockets; radios of all sorts, portable tellies, fur coats, cameras, binoculars – oh hell, there were so many things on show that I'd waste your time if I tried to list them all. But I love to look at things of beauty and I spent a lot of time looking for looking's sake. I bent over the exhibits, giving them a close and loving scrutiny but knowing very well that I'd never seen any of this stuff before. Who had nicked it all I couldn't imagine, but it was fairly clear that the ungodly had been working overtime recently.

Several more people came in – more genuine in their quest than I had been – and I heard one middle-aged lady squeal with joy as she clutched a model sail boat done in jewelled mother-of-pearl.

"Oh, officer, this is mine," she said. "My dear late husband brought it for me, all the way from Australia."

One of the jacks advanced on her, looking stern.

"If you'll step this way, madam, we'll have a little talk."

He stalked out of the room with the old dear in his wake and I decided it was time for me to leave. I'd have to find a phone kiosk somewhere and link up with Boggis that way. Not too close to the nick, though. Better to ring up from some distance away. I began to move towards the exit, casting a last lingering look at some of the goodies on show, and just before I came to the end of the table there was a creak and a shuffle and Boggis came in.

He saw me straight away and, typically, turned his nose in the air, ignoring me in the most obvious way imaginable. Evidently he meant to give me the full treatment, for he swung right at a gap between tables and headed for the corner of the room farthest away from me. But if Boggis wants to score that way, he'll have to wait till I'm asleep. I followed him, cutting him off, and when I had him more or less trapped I grabbed the nearest item from the nearest table – a rather ugly looking ornament, it was – and waved it at him.

"Oh, officer, officer," I said. "I think this is mine."

*   *   *

I could tell the volcano was about to explode by the set of Bert's face (which bore all the friendliness of a haddock's) by the snap in his voice when he acknowledged my plea and by the vibrations set up in the floorboards as he marched out of the room with me tagging dutifully along in his wake. But he stayed calm all the way through the building and up the stairs until the door of his office closed behind us. He even offered me a seat, no doubt for the benefit of anybody looking in. There is a small window to the right of his desk, through which passing jacks can cast glances. But once I'd parked my bottom and eased my pants legs he blew his top in that quiet, controlled way he has, that's designed to keep the row local and stop other wagging ears joining in.

"You despicable little turd," he hissed. "You stand there and show me up in front of my men. You don't take the slightest bloody notice of all the warnings I've given you. I say keep away, you come flashing your face for everyone to see. I ask the public to help me, and what turns up? A piece of gutter sludge who never should have oozed out of the bloody sewer – you, you slimy little sod. And then you pick up a nice vase – nicer than anything you could ever afford in all your rotten little puff – and you claim it for your own. I should charge you with theft, you light fingered little creep. Anyway, why have you come here? To what do we owe the honour?"

But I wasn't taking a great deal of notice. I was staring goggle eyed at an item that lay on the blotter on Bert's desk. I pointed a quavering finger and waited till he stopped, then I said:

"What the hell's that?"

"I'm sick of the sight of you, Peeper," he went on. "There was a time when you could be useful, but you've lost the knack in your old age. Nowadays you never come in with a bloody thing worth knowing. You just get in my way – waste my time. I wash my bloody hands of you. Get out. Go away. Don't bother me any more."

"But what is it, for God's sake? Where did you get it?"

At last he deigned to look where I was looking. He picked the item up, dangled it on one of his fingers.

"Are you stupid or something? It's a gun."

"I can see it's a gun, Bert. It's a Smith and Wesson point three-eight revolver, but that's not what I mean. What I mean is, what great feat of detection does it represent? In which earth-shattering case is it the vital clue? What mayhem has been done with that gun to make it of interest to an awe-inspiring sod like you? Put in simpler terms – where did you get the bloody thing?"

"No business of yours," he said shortly.

"But I think it is. I've got a very strong gut-feeling about it. I saw something like that very recently and I'm anxious to know whether it's the same one. So don't be such a bloody stuffed-shirt, Bert Boggis. Spit it out, man – let's all enjoy it."

"The uniform lads brought it in during the night. Took it off one of our local hooks. It's still under investigation."

"Somebody they picked up for speeding?" I questioned coyly.

Boggis looked hard at me and his eyes glittered. I waited for a spirited reply but I didn't get any reply at all, so I tried again.

"Or maybe it wasn't for speeding, Bert. Maybe it was for driving a Mini in a dangerous manner, without regard for other road users."

"You're pretty clever at guessing games," he said sourly.

"All right. Let me have a go at possible extra charges. Being too fat to fit in a Mini, shall we say? Using four-letter words when spoken to by the officer? Or maybe it was more simple than that, Bert. A clear case of indecent exposure, shall we say?"

His look had become a glare. He was very very annoyed.

"You do know something, you little bastard," he conceded. "But that still doesn't make it your business. All that does is make me very suspicious of you. So I'm waiting for an explanation. What the hell do you know about the events of last night?"

"It was Bunker Hunker, wasn't it."

"Suppose it was – what of it?"

"He nearly shot me with that bloody thing, that's what. I'm here to make a complaint against Bunker – assault with a deadly weapon, is that what you call it? I'm lucky to be alive, Bert."

The anger had gone out of his face, to be replaced by avarice.

"Maybe you can help after all, Peeper," he said.

"I'm a bit short of evidence on that bastard Bunker. Found in possession of a firearm, I can make that stick all right, but maybe there's more."

"Driving with no clothes on?" I suggested.

"Not as serious as it sounds," Boggis said without a hint of humour. "No females to be insulted, no other people around to make it a public exposure. The traffic lads wouldn't have seen him if they hadn't stopped the car and looked in. No, you can forget all about nude driving. Mind you, Peeper," his nose began to twitch and there were several little nerves having spasms on his face, "it'll take old Bunker a while to live it down. The word's gone round like wildfire. Everybody knows about it."

"But it won't get in the papers?"

"No. No chance. Between you and me, Peeper, if there was an offence, I'd charge him with it just to watch the bugger squirm."

"Have you thought about kidnapping?"

He flashed me a very startled but wary look.

"Kidnapping? Whatever are you on about?"

"The Bernadette woman. That's where they took her. God damn it, man, don't tell me you haven't even searched Bunker's house?"

"The traffic lads have. They did it straight away. Not just Bunker's house either. They did nearly the whole terrace."

"Is that Parkview Terrace, off the old road?"

"That's it – the rat gallery."

"Then you're about twenty miles out of date, Bert. That's where he used to live. Maybe he's still using that address, but he's got another. Bunker's a married man now, remember, and a father. He married Jane Prendergast and knocked one off the shelf for her.

Don't tell me you didn't know he had a nice new house."

"Where is it at?"

I told him.

"How long has he been living there?"

"How should I know? I only found out yesterday."

"And you say that's where they took Mrs O'Mahoney?"

"That's right, Bert. Middle bedroom at the back."

"How the hell did you find that out, Peeper?"

"I did it for you, Bert. You asked me to find out."

"Yes, you little sod, and I also asked you to tell me. Why the hell didn't you tell me?"

"I'm telling you now, Bert," I said, suppressing a chuckle.

*   *   *

It strikes me, sometimes, that I'm not as fair with Boggis as I might be. I'm always accusing him of looking down on me, spurning me, treating me like something the dog left on the doorstep, but deep down he trusts me implicitly. He must do, or he wouldn't have gone haring out of the office, leaving me in full possession of all his official property and records, not to mention an ugly looking vase from his display and a loaded revolver. Mind you, he put me firmly on my honour to behave myself and treat the contents of his office with the care they deserved. "Move a muscle and I'll geld you, you little sod," was the way he put it.

So I did as I was told. Several nosy jacks and a couple of quite nice-looking secretaries bobbed into the office in the hour or so that followed, but they all bobbed out again without asking me who I was or why I was there. And eventually Boggis himself returned. I tried to read his face, to find out whether he was pleased or not. I couldn't tell. He has the sort of face that gives very little away.

"Was your journey really necessary?" I asked.

"They've shifted her," he said bitterly. "Oh she was there all right. We've found bits of her clothing and her membership card from the health centre. But she's not there any more."

"I could have told you that before you set out, Bert," I said.

"You could? Then why the bloody hell didn't you?"

"You never asked me," I said.

            ※   ※   ※

After that we got down to brass tacks, as we usually do once we've got all the sparring out of the way. Boggis told me about the raid on Bunker's house. It was partially successful. The signs of occupation by a pregnant female – almost certainly Bernadette O'Mahoney – were strong enough for him to consider charges of kidnapping and, as he pointed out, once the O'Mahoney woman emerged from cover to give evidence, the case would be stronger. But there were other matters of interest. The search team had found another revolver, a small quantity of gelignite and an assortment of stolen property, so even without the kidnapping charge he had enough to hold the people from the house.

"Two men and a woman, Bert?" I suggested.

"And don't forget the child, Peeper. The Prendergast woman, I'm damned if I can call her Hunker, brought so many nappies into custody with her my car looked like a bloody market stall. Between you and me, that baby's a flaming nuisance. She's got it with her in one of the female cells, with half our female staff hanging around to satisfy her slightest whim. There's baby bottles all over the shop. They'll have bloody washing lines strung around before they've done."

"And the two blokes?"

"Fairly new. Ellis Neale and George Humphry. Humphry's a stranger to me. I've met Neale before, when he was in the dock at Crown court a while back But they're both villains, Peeper, and they'll both get the hammer if I can arrange it." He paused and gave me a long look. "And now it's your turn, you devious bugger. What have you done with Bernadette O'Mahoney?"

"She's safe as houses, Bert," I told him. I thought he might be pleased to hear it, but he certainly didn't look pleased.

"I don't wish to know that, Peeper. There's only one agency paid to look after victims of crime, and that's the police. So don't give me that guff about how safe she is. Where the hell is she, and how soon can you bring her here?"

"Bring her here? Bollocks. You must be out of your mind."

He didn't fly off the handle straight away. He would eventually, of course, but to start with he forced himself to use sweet reason.

"I don't see what's bothering you, Peeper. The poor woman's been through quite an ordeal. All she wants is to be restored to the bosom of her family – now what could be more simple than that?"

"The only bosoms in Bernadette's family are right there with her," I said. "If you mean she wishes to be reunited with her husband, well there's some truth in that. But she doesn't want to finish up in a cell – and that's where Terrence O'Mahoney is at the moment."

"Who says he is?" Boggis was waxing belligerent.

"I do. And she does. And that's where he is." I gave him a grimace that said I was fed up of being pissed about by him. "It's time for the cards on the table bit. You think I can't read the signs? You've got Terrence O'Mahoney here, and he's grassing like mad. At any rate, he was grassing like mad till Bunker Hunker stopped his mouth by snatching Bernadette. We can get together on this, Bert, you and I. I've taken the pressure off your supergrass by snatching his wife back off the snatchers, but I don't work for nothing, and I don't work in the dark. Now let's have the story. Tell me where we stand. And maybe when we understand each other, things can start to happen."

"Just suppose you happened to be right," Boggis sneered. "What sort of a cop do you take me for? Nobody knows better than you, how important it is never to betray a confidence. Whether O'Mahoney's working for me or not is neither here nor there. The point is, it's none of your business and I don't intend to discuss it."

"You're afraid he'll be blown? Don't make me laugh, Bert, it hurts my shoulders. Terrence was blown high wide and handsome a long time ago. Why the hell do you suppose they kidnapped Bernadette? But you know the reason for that, of course, because that was the form the ransom note took, even though you deny having received one. And until you convince Terrence that Bernadette's O.K. you're in deep trouble. He certainly won't tell you any more – and almost certainly he'll go back on what he's said already. Forget about ethics with friend Terrence O'Mahoney. Play your cards my way. Re-unite him with his missus, then play him out in the open. Milk him of everything he's got. Shove him in the witness box. Then, when it's all over, pull a few strings and get him transported with his wife and baby to some place where they can live happily ever after."

I knew I'd won Boggis to my side. He was going to confide in me. But like many another spoilt brat he's never prepared to give in until he's explored every silly little angle. He made his mind up to come the heavy. It never works – but he never learns.

"You stand in exactly the same place as the kidnappers," he said. "If I find you have this woman hidden away, I shall charge you with abducting her – and you'll never talk your way out of it."

"All right then. Find her."

"I won't have to look far. A search warrant for the Albion Hotel should be all I require. You've got her lodged there, with that fat cow, Stella. You can't fool me, Peeper."

He watched me very carefully as he said this, waiting for me to betray the twinge of concern that would tell him he'd guessed right. I didn't twinge. I just grinned at him.

"Go to the Albion," I said. "Search to your heart's content."

Bert Boggis was very leery then, for reasons well known to both of us. But it's not fair if you don't know the reason too, so let me explain. I've already told you about Stella and her zeal for reform. Another very pronounced facet of her character is the deep hatred she feels for policemen. I haven't the slightest idea how it started, but I suspect some copper must have done her wrong way back in her youth. In my more sombre moments I sometimes wonder if that copper was Boggis, but although I've suggested as much to him he always denies it. The only thing I'm really sure of is the existence of the hatred. She never loses it. In fact it gets stronger every day. And Boggis has good reason to know about it, because he's tangled with her a couple of times and come away with tail between legs.

Once, many years ago when I'd only just met Stella and knew no better, I sent Boggis along to interview her about something or other. She listened to him till he said the magic words 'I'm a police officer' and then she frog-marched him to the front door and threw him down the steps. Since then, the only reason why he hasn't set her place on fire and charged her with arson is because I've pleaded with him not to.

So I knew very well Boggis was bluffing. He wouldn't go to the Albion with any warrant – not even if he believed Bernadette was there.

"I'll get a ticket for your house, then," he said.

"Don't bother with a ticket, Bert," I said. "Just go and have a look round. I'll give you full authority and there'll be no talk of suing you when you find nothing. Do me a favour, old mate. Would I bother Doreen with a cocked up job like this?"

"No. You surely wouldn't," he said, thus displaying what a fool he can be sometimes. "So what have you done with her, Peeper? I want her back. I've got to have her."

"The mountain won't come to Mahomet," I said. "So what you have to arrange is a transfer in the opposite direction."

"If you're trying to make a suggestion," he said, "give it to me in plain English."

"Let's have a meeting point," I said. "I'll bring my party, you bring yours, and they can get together on neutral ground."

"Take a prisoner out of the nick? Are you raving mad?"

"He is a prisoner then. You do admit it?"

"Never mind what I admit. Stay with this stupid suggestion of yours. How much do you think my job's worth? I'm a detective sergeant. Do you think I'd risk my position by taking a prisoner out of a cell on the say-so of a little snot like you, and dragging him up and down the place just to meet people?"

"Yes." I said.

"And where would we go to have this meeting?"

"Well, let me think a bit."

I thought rather a lot to be quite honest. I didn't have anything planned because I hadn't been sure that Boggis would agree. Come to that, I didn't even know whether Bernadette would agree, but somehow I believed she would. So I had to do my thinking from scratch – and the first place I thought of was Frenchy Watts's house. Parrott and his mates were still in custody and I knew the place was empty because I'd been in there quite recently and done a check. I almost suggested the Watts place, till I had another last minute idea.

"You locked up the whole caboodle at Bunker's place?" I asked.

"Everything that moved," he said.

"That's it, then. We'll meet at Bunker's house."

"What time? Don't make it later than two – I've something on then."

"Two? I was thinking of later than that. I was thinking of tomorrow. I need time to make the arrangements, Bert. Let's make it tomorrow – mid morning –

say eleven o'clock."

"Eleven o'clock it is," he said.

I was completely nonplussed. I reckon to understand Bert Boggis fairly well, whatever his mood, but this mood of acquiescence was something completely foreign to his nature and therefore good grounds for healthy suspicion.

"I hope this is a genuine offer on your part, Boggis," I said. "No tricks, now. Because if you try to pull anything fancy on me, the deal's off."

"Don't be ridiculous, Peeper. What tricks could I pull?"

"I'm damned if I know, but I'll think about it. Why didn't you argue? What's so special about eleven o'clock that made you accept it without question? I don't trust you, Boggis."

"You'll have to trust me, Peeper. I'll have Terrence O'Mahoney there. You have his wife there and all will be well."

"O.K., Bert, I'm relying on you." I picked up the vase I'd taken from display and held it out to him. "You'd better put this back where I found it, Bert, and you'd better escort me out that way. It would never do for people to think I was anything but a witness."

* * *

He showed me off the premises like a good 'un. I waved him a big cheerio, walked away for a couple of streets, then called him up from a phone box. He was panting a little. He must have just got back to his office from seeing me off.

"Don't worry about the gun, Bert," I said. "I won't use it and I won't lose it."

"I'm going to see you get time for that," Boggis

fumed. "That's a straight theft from a police station."

"Nothing of the sort, Bert," I countered. "It's insurance. Just make sure you play it straight tomorrow, old mate, and after that you can have your gun back."

ELEVEN

The life of a police informer is fraught with danger at the best of times, and never more so than when he has a meeting and the most delicate negotiations to arrange. I'd fixed thing with Boggis, but making the rest of it run smoothly was quite a problem.

Reaching an agreement with Bernadette was relatively simple. She took a stand against sneaking back into the house she'd so recently sneaked out of, but when I casually mentioned that this time it would be Terrence – not Bunker – who awaited her, she accepted with alacrity. Doreen was less easy to convince. In the Bernadette O'Mahoney case I'd involved Doreen more than she had ever been involved in any previous escapade – and whilst she'd rather dragged herself into this one and enjoyed the adventure it had so far brought her, she was nearing the stage where enough of a good thing is enough. But I had to have Doreen. I certainly didn't intend to go haring about the town unchaperoned with somebody else's wife in tow. So I pointed out to Doreen that she had landed me in this particular pickle and that it was up to her to wiggle me out.

Having worked successfully on Doreen, I faced the only remaining problem. It was the most dangerous problem of all – how to transport self and two women across the heart of a hostile town quickly, easily and without letting too many people see. I'm not afraid of danger. I'd made a lifetime's habit of solving problems. I solved this one.

I nicked a car.

It was a car I'd kept up my sleeve (metaphorically, that is) for just such an emergency. The owner had a job on an oil rig somewhere in the North Sea and a wife who made the most of his absences with a bloke who ran a bigger and better car. The fancy bloke's Mercedes was parked outside the front of her house, so I went to a croft at the top of the street and climbed into the neglected Vauxhall Viva.

I couldn't hope to hide the girls and myself in such a car, but I used my knowledge of the town to follow a quiet route, and when we arrived in the alley behind Bunker's house I was pretty sure we hadn't been seen. Maybe I should point out, at this stage, that the risks I was running were considerably more than the average. When a thief nicks a car he must look out for two enemies – the owner and the cops. When I nicked this particular car I knew the owner would be no risk at all, but I had to watch for the cops and also *for every mobster in town who had reason to fear Terrence and Bernadette O'Mahoney*, and that must have worked out at a tidy old total. The risks didn't end there. Apart from facing 'the cops' in general, I also had to watch out for my own personal cop. Boggis does have a certain amount of discretion – his eye works as Nelson's is reputed to have done – but if I were ever mad enough to let him actually catch me committing crime – let him see me with a stolen car – I knew damned well he'd carry out his oft repeated threat and feel my collar officially.

But everything had gone well so far. We climbed the gate and traipsed up to the back of Bunker's house. No need to climb on the roof this time – I just eased a window on the ground floor and shoved Doreen through to slip the catch on the door and let us in. Boggis hadn't arrived yet – well, I'd deliberately come early because if a meeting is in any way potentially dangerous it pays to get there ahead of the opposition. I steered Doreen and Bernadette upstairs to the back bedroom, then came down again and stood in the front room, peeping out through the half drawn curtains and watching the street.

I saw Bert's old banger draw up at the kerb outside – and straight away there was something I didn't like. Bert climbed out and walked up the path to the front door. The bloke following in his wake could only be Terrence O'Mahoney. I was seeing Terrence for the first time. He turned out to be youngish, younger than Bernadette I'd have guessed, and surprisingly slightly built. He was wearing a black pin striped suit, (woefully out of style or bang up to the latest fashion, I didn't know which) that was cut slim, so that the trousers were almost tight. He had light, bushy hair that made his head look too large for his body – a half-sucked lollipop with a black stick. But it wasn't O'Mahoney that caused me concern – it was the third member of the party, a young copper in full uniform.

I stared at the copper in disgust – and I was still staring at him when a taxi drew past the house, slowly, hesitantly, before picking up speed and drawing away. I mention the taxi because it has a certain importance. At the time, the only thing important to me was the copper.

You brainless crapbag, Boggis, I silently told myself. *Of all the things you don't do, trust you to bloody well do it. If there was ever a time when a copper was an unnecessary luxury, this is it.*

Once again, I'd slightly misjudged the man. No

power on earth could have made me go to the door and let him in, but I didn't have to. He used a key (borrowed from Bunker's property bag, no doubt) and I heard the trio come into the hall. The front room door opened, Boggis slipped in alone and closed the door after him.

"Where are they?" he hissed.

"Take your silver-buttoned friend to hell out of here, Bert."

"Never mind him. Keep out of the way and he won't see you. Where've you put Mrs. O'Mahoney?"

"Middle back bedroom, upstairs, Doreen's with her."

"All right, then. This won't take long, Peeper. You hang about in here till I've sorted things out, then I'll slip downstairs and let you know. Incidentally, I might be taking her back with me."

"Bernadette? Over my dead body you will."

"Don't be stupid. I've reason to believe she'll want to go with her husband. If she does, I shall take her."

I would have protested louder and longer if I hadn't known it would be a waste of time. If Boggis had been on his own I might have risked a trial of strength, but there was an honest to goodness proper policeman with him, and that threw the scales right over. Besides, Bernadette was becoming a bit of a liability, and in common humanity she was entitled to do what the hell she liked with her freedom.

"If she wants to go, so be it," I said. "But not till I've heard it from her own lips. So if you decide you're going to take her, Boggis, I want to be in on the conference."

"You don't want to be in on any conference, Peeper. You don't want my constable to see you. Come to that, it's probably safer if O'Mahoney doesn't see you."

"That's all right. Bring Bernadette. I'll talk to her alone."

☆   ☆   ☆

And now, let me bring your mind back to that taxi.

As I told you once before, I have the sort of memory that picks up things without realising it, then trots out the information later. Standing by the front window in Bunker's house, staring moodily out while I waited for Boggis to complete his business upstairs, I saw the taxi again. It was parked maybe a hundred yards away along the street and two people had climbed out of it. Of these two, one was carrying the other, and the one being carried was in the category known as 'very tiny'. I think it's fair to say that I recognised young Gary Hunker even before I recognised his mother, but it can only have been a split second afterwards that I recognised Jane Hunker, nee Prendergast. I was surprised to see her. I'd had every reason to believe she was safely locked away in the hoosegow. I wondered how a woman like her could have managed to bend bars, break glass bricks and climb out of a cell window carrying a baby.

Fool that I was, I attached no great importance to the arrival of Jane Prendergast. I could read the picture as easy as pie. She'd come home in a taxi and seen a battered old Ford Consul parked outside her house and without needing to call on the wisdom of the ages she'd conjectured that the visitor in her absence was Detective Sergeant Albert Boggis. So she'd retired to a respectful distance, and now she proposed to wait there until Boggis left. I couldn't quite figure out why she hadn't sent the taxi packing – if his meter was still ticking away she was likely to run up a hefty bill – but maybe she had money to burn, and maybe …? That was when my memory threw up the information about when I'd first seen the taxi.

It had been cruising past the house at the precise moment of Bert's arrival. It followed, therefore, that Prendergast hadn't only seen a car belonging to Boggis, she'd seen Boggis himself. She'd also seen a policeman – and she'd seen Terrence O'Mahoney.

Did Prendergast know Terrence O'Mahoney?

It was an intriguing question – and I couldn't see any way of checking the answer without causing painful repercussions. If she didn't know O'Mahoney there was little harm done, but if she *did* know him, things might be very dicey indeed.

Even then, I didn't feel over much alarm. Assuming the worst, that she knew O'Mahoney and would read a lot of truth into what she had just seen, what harm could Prendergast do? She was a woman – and not a very robust woman at that – and without any backing she didn't pose much of a threat. So to hell with Prendergast. I made a mental note to mention her presence to Boggis – and that was all I did.

Until I looked again and saw that the taxi had gone. Moreover, Jane Prendergast and her offspring had gone with it. I knew a minute or two of complete ease, when I recognised that even the remote chance of interference had receded, but they were wasted minutes. When I began to take notice again the taxi was back in the street – and either it had had rapid growing pups or two other cars had joined it. The two new arrivals – a black Rover and a cream Ford – were not taxis, but they seemed to be part of the same convoy. As I watched, Prendergast climbed out of the taxi – without her baby now – and several rough looking blokes climbed out of the cars and joined her.

At least two of the men were familiar faces – Frank Toppin and Sam (Tellie) Taylor – and I thought I'd seen a couple of the others somewhere before. They stood there, admiring Bert's Consul and I waited to see what they would do.

I felt pretty certain they hadn't seen me. There was no light in Bunker's front room and I'd stayed pretty close to the curtains all the time. But if they decided to storm the house they'd see me then, and the thought made me distinctly uncomfortable. But they didn't seem to be making any move – so maybe their plan was still the same – to wait till Boggis packed up and left. I glanced idly towards my right – along the street in the opposite direction. There was just one car. A neighbour's car, parked there in all innocence? It didn't seem likely. Not with Smithy and Fred Head standing by it.

It was a time to throw caution to the winds – a time not to give a bugger any more whether the copper saw me or not. I shot upstairs, threw the bedroom door open and gabbled my message to Boggis. He joined me in the front room and peered at the gathering scene.

"They've bailed her," he said. "I was half afraid they would, what with her having a baby with her and all. The charge wasn't all that serious against her. They've stuck the other two in custody and bailed the Prendergast woman. Damn it to hell, Peeper. That could make things very awkward indeed."

"You should grumble Bert. Imagine where it puts me."

"Blast you for a whining coward, Peeper. I don't give a shit about you – or me either, for that matter. They're not after us, man. They're after Terrence O'Mahoney. And it sticks out like a gut on a goitre –

they know I've got him here."

"What's to be done, Bert," I asked, my voice reduced to a whisper by the onset of the most dreadful funk.

"I'm thinking," he said. "And if you want to make yourself useful, Peeper, you start thinking too."

⁕   ⁕   ⁕

I don't claim all the credit for the solution we worked out. Boggis does, but Boggis is a shameless and acquisitive liar. To be fair, we should share the credit with the young uniformed copper who also chucked in his two-pennorth. What I *can* say is that Bernadette didn't like it, and Doreen didn't like it – and Terrence O'Mahoney wasn't thrilled about it either.

"Come on," I said to Terrence, having completely misunderstood his reluctance to remove his trousers, "the girls have seen one before."

"Up yours," he said in his lilting Irish brogue. "I strongly object to changing clothes with a tart."

I strongly objected to him calling Doreen a tart – and so did Doreen, I might say – but this was no time to haggle about niceties. With Boggis rushing around like a dog herding sheep we had troubles enough to contend with, and very little time.

So I swallowed my pride and got on with the dress rehearsal. Within minutes, Boggis was queueing up at the door ready to leave, with the young copper in third man position and Doreen – in dark pin stripes with her hair mussed out like a dandelion – playing monkey (or Terrence O'Mahoney) in the middle. Watching them go, we the rearguard were very impressed. Boggis and the copper were quite unmistakable and they herded round Doreen in a protective way. Even at our distance

– and we were much closer than the watching mob – Doreen was a ringer for Terrence. All three of them climbed into Bert's Consul. The Consul moved away. There was a scattering of figures alongside the other cars. Within seconds a black Rover and a cream Ford were tailing along behind the Consul. I watched Fred Head's car do a swift three point and tag on behind. For the car-conscious reader, Fred was driving an oldish looking Vauxhall Carlton.

*   *   *

They vanished from sight, and I have to rely on hearsay in order to tell you what happened next. But I believe you ought to have the story at this stage, so here goes.

After maybe a quarter of a mile, the Rover overtook the Consul, pulled in in front and slowed down. Boggis slowed down even more until there was a gap between him and the Rover, whereupon the Ford overtook Boggis and pulled into the gap. At that stage it was hard to tell what these bastards had in mind. They'd be reluctant, Boggis reasoned, to openly attack a car carrying two policemen, one in uniform, but a lot depended on how desperate they were to have a go at Terrence O'Mahoney. It was pretty safe to conclude that they still believed the third person in the car was O'Mahoney – Doreen had kept her head well down and was showing all the signs of not wanting to be seen – and there were a few quiet by-ways to pass along before Boggis and crew reached safety. Rather than wait and see, Boggis decided to bring matters to a head. He braked hard, swung the Consul into the kerb and stopped. Fred Head, following behind in his Vauxhall Carlton, swerved and narrowly missed colliding with the Consul before coming to a stop half-way alongside it. The Rover and the cream Ford stopped some distance ahead, then both cars reversed till they were directly in front of the Consul. The trap was sprung, but there were plenty of houses about and Boggis was not feeling greatly scared. He and the uniformed constable climbed out and strolled round to the Carlton. Boggis opened the driver's door.

Boggis: "That was a bit of shocking driving, Fred."

Fred Head: "Come on, Sergeant. Do us a favour. It was you, braking like that. I never had a chance."

Boggis: "Do your duty, Constable."

Constable: "Can I see your driving licence, sir?"

Fred Head: "I've left the bugger at home."

Constable: "In that case, sir …"

And without going too far into detail, suffice it to say that the constable went through all the tedious motions of reporting Fred Head for driving without due care and attention and – incidentally – for having no tax or insurance.

Whilst this was proceeding, Boggis and the constable pointedly ignored the Rover and the cream Ford. But the occupants of those other cars were hopping about like demented fleas and first one, then another, would climb out, edge his way along the pavement towards the Consul, crane his neck and go back to report. Things began to appear a little nasty when the one became three – and at that stage, Boggis decided to play his next card. He advanced on the advancers.

Boggis: "Can I help you, gentlemen?"

Shark Sharkey: "Just taking the air, Sergeant, and having a look at your car. It's weathered well, but there's too many rust patches. I reckon it's time you invested in a new one, and as it happens I've got just the car for you."

(Let it be known, that Reginald (Shark) Sharkey, besides being a local crook in the trusted lieutenant bracket, is also a used car salesman of dubious reputation.)

> *Boggis*: "No thanks, Shark. There's a mile or two in her yet."
>
> *Sharkey*: "Just the same, I'd like to look her over. These old Consuls were well made. They seem to go on for ever. Mind if I check the upholstery?"
>
> *Boggis*: "Help yourself, so long as you don't molest my secretary." (He advanced to the Consul) "Just step out a minute, Miss Jackson. The gentleman wants to take a look."

Whereupon, Doreen stuck her head up and stepped out of the car into full view, giving Sharkey and company the benefit of her peach cheeks, her fluttering lashes, her well-rouged lips and her smartly feminine masculine attire. Exit Shark Sharkey and his mates. They withdrew in utter confusion, leaving Fred Head to his fate. A minute or two later, Head left the scene with tail between legs and Boggis, Doreen and the young copper were back in command. The journey proceeded and – for the moment at least – all was well.

※　※　※

Meantime, back at Bunker's place, things were going less well, though I must hasten to add that our difficulties were mere nuisance. Terrence O'Mahoney point blank refused to dress himself up in Doreen's blouse and fetching little skirt. I didn't much blame him – they wouldn't have looked half so well on him as they did on Doreen – but as I pointed out, they would at least preserve the niceties of decency whilst we spirited him away.

But he wouldn't have it – and we finished up scouring Bunker's wardrobes for something more suitable. A pair of slacks – too small for Bunker or either of his mates – turned up in a drawer, and those he agreed to wear, but the only thing we could find to complete his ensemble was a turtle neck sweater that – on Terrence – looked like an off-the-shoulder woollen dress and had to be worn rolled up in a tyre about his middle. Still, it was enough to get us started. We nipped down the back garden and I drove away with both Terrence and Bernadette crouching low in the back seat.

By far the hairiest moment was in the back street behind the Albion Hotel. I had to risk leaving the Viva there, much as I disliked the idea of bringing Stella's establishment into disrepute. As soon as I could, I nipped out and drove it back to where I'd found it, but before then I'd spoken to Stella and fixed things up.

Stella lashed out the tea and scones in her usual hospitable fashion and didn't want to know too much about the new guests I was wishing on her. But she did have one reservation, and when the chance came she whispered the gist in my earhole.

"Poor woman. She shouldn't be here, James. She should be in hospital. Any minute now we shall have one of nature's miracles."

"She'll be all right, Stella," I told her. "Bernadette's not due for a day or two, and by then I'll have her out of here. This is only temporary. They've fallen on hard times."

"You mean they're not able to pay? That doesn't matter, James. They look trustworthy. I don't mind giving credit for a while."

"They'll pay all right. I mean they've had problems with accommodation. All they want is a room for a couple of nights."

"They are married, aren't they? I mean – booking one room, they've got to be husband and wife. I shouldn't like to think ..."

"Oh for God's sake, Stella. Everything's on the up and up, I tell you. Now leave everything to me and stop worrying."

✳ ✳ ✳

Putting the car away took rather a long time, and when I came back I found a state of affairs in the O'Mahoney bedroom that I can only describe as an 'atmosphere'. Bernadette was crouched in a chair, sobbing, and Terrence was lying on the bed, kicking hell out of a pillow. I interceded, feeling anxious. It only took my tentative 'What's up?' to get Terrence really going.

"I'll tear the bastard up, sure I will," he said. "I'll make mincemeat of the bugger. Just let me at him. I'll punch him on the nose, I'll twist his clack till he throttles, I'll take that big nose of his and rip it off his face. I'll ..."

There was a great deal more of this and I listened sympathetically. Gradually it dawned on me that he was talking about Bunker. Bunker Hunker had had the temerity to lay hands on Bernadette. He'd slapped her face. In doing so, he'd incurred the undying wrath of Terrence O'Mahoney. The cause of Bernadette's upset was closely related. She'd told her husband the story of Bunker's assault, and now, because Terrence had taken it so badly, she was regretting having shot her mouth off.

I considered the position. There was a humorous angle to the notion of O'Mahoney laying hands on

Bunker, 'tearing the bastard up' and 'twisting his clack till he throttles', but I kept my face straight. I knew Terrence didn't think it was a joke. Small as Terrence was, I got the feeling that I wouldn't want him as an enemy.

I stayed with them until Boggis telephoned – and that call came a great deal later than expected. I took the call, but Boggis wanted Terrence, so I handed over. They talked for quite a long time, and when the call ended, Terrence was flaming mad about something. He wanted to tell me there and then, but I shushed him along until we were back in the bedroom and Stella couldn't hear. Then he began to rave. "The bastards. the bastards. The lousy bastards …"

I let him get on with it, and after a while he calmed down enough to say to me. "I've got to go. Sergeant Boggis is sending a car. He won't come here. He wants you to take me out and meet him round the corner. He says you'll know the place.

"Can't you stay tonight, love?" Bernadette wailed.

"No. I must go."

"Can't we just go home and stay there?"

"Home?" he snapped. "You mean to our lovely house with all our lovely furniture? We're never going there again."

"Why not?" she asked, faltering.

"Because they burned the bugger down, this afternoon."

*   *   *

The man I escorted from the Albion Hotel to his rendezvous with Bert Boggis was a very angry man indeed. Merely by walking with him and feeling the vibes as they coiled about him I learned the answer to a question that had always puzzled me before – namely, why be a supergrass? I'm not one of those – and never shall be – and the distinction is not fine, it's broad and hairy. Terrence O'Mahoney and I had nothing in common at all, apart that is from our tendency to speak to policemen about villains. With me it was a living, something I did all the time – regardless of who might be involved – simply to earn as much reward money as possible. With O'Mahoney it was more personal. He'd gone ape for some reason. He'd fallen out with his erstwhile buddies and embarked on a crusade to see them all in hell. I always had to be so careful not to become 'blown' but O'Mahoney didn't give much of a damn. He certainly didn't care now, after the hate he'd built up against Bunker Hunker.

As I walked away, leaving him with Boggis, I was very glad O'Mahoney knew nothing detrimental about me.

*   *   *

But I should say in passing that I didn't get away from Boggis as easy as that. He actually got out of his car and grabbed me by the front of my shirt.

"Before I forget," he said smoothly. "you've got something of mine and I want the bugger back."

"You mean the gun, Bert?" I said, in all innocence.

"That's right. Now hand the bugger over and we'll say no more."

"Sorry, Bert. Can't do that. I haven't got it, you see. I hate the bloody nasty things. You won't find me toting a gun around town. I simply won't do it."

"Where the hell is it, then. Come on Peeper. This is serious."

"Try your book-case, Bert," I said. "Third shelf down. Right behind Stone's Justices' Manual."

TWELVE

I never saw Terrence O'Mahoney again.

But in case you think you've seen something sinister in the way I said that, let me reassure you. Far from fading into obscurity he blossomed like a rose. Thinking back, the public exposure of O'Mahoney – and to a lesser extent his wife – dates from when I took him out of the Albion Hotel and handed him over to Bert Boggis.

Almost immediately, the effects of their association began to be felt. If there had been a reduction in the criminal population a few weeks earlier it was as nothing to the flood of arrests that occurred in the next few days. And this time the element of secrecy was not present. Terrence O'Mahoney began to appear in court, on a regular basis, to give evidence against every sort of rogue for every class of crime in the book. The Crown Court lists grew longer and longer as more and more people were committed to stand trial.

You'll have noticed it was Terrence I never saw again. I saw Bernadette again, several times. She spent less than twenty-four hours at the Albion, and then an ambulance arrived and she was taken away. I'm one of the few people, outside the police, who know the location of the nursing home to which Bernadette was taken, and wild horses wouldn't drag that information out of me. One of the others (the people outside the police who know, etc ...) is Doreen. She and I went several times, under close escort and quite free of charge, to the place I wouldn't tell wild horses about, and a few days later young Janine Welsh O'Mahoney was born. (Don't ask me about that middle name – I haven't a clue.) Mother and child did well, as they say, and they stayed there for nearly a month. After that they moved on under a cloak of secrecy. Do I know where they went to? I won't say. What I will say is that I still receive news of them, and of Terrence, and they're all doing well. But once again I'm getting too far ahead of myself. I have an awful lot of ground to cover, even if I only cover it briefly.

With things happening all around us, Doreen and I retired from public life, though the retirement was only temporary. We spent our time reading newspapers, watching telly and doing our damnedest to keep abreast of events. We had a vested interest. There was a real danger that we might be called as witnesses, and that would not have been a pleasant thing to happen.

I was pleased to see that amongst the people re-arrested as a result of O'Mahoney's new disclosures were all those who had been released without charge following Bernadette's kidnapping and its retarding effect on her husband's tongue. Alistair (Swanky Alice) Proud, Bent Nelson and John Field paid the price for their raid on Crewe's betting shop, as well as for other matters. Lenny Bethel, Chester Moreland, Big Ginger Fish and Peter David Parrott collected long sentences. So did Fred Head, Smithy and Harold Gavin (Cutter) Watson. Shark Sharkey and half a dozen others were brought into the net, and for his little clash with Bert Boggis, Fred Head had an extra appearance at the lower court for traffic offences.

Bunker Hunker, Jane Prendergast, Ellis Neale and George Humphry were eventually convicted on a variety of charges, but the charge which most caught the imagination of the public was that of abducting Bernadette O'Mahoney. Bernadette revelled in her day and her acid Irish tongue was more than enough to put the finishing touches to an otherwise fairly thin case. This was the case which most closely involved Doreen and myself, and I have to admit we worried about it. But as it happened, our evidence was not required and all four were found guilty.

That case against Bunker and his accomplices was Bernadette's last public appearance before she departed for places unknown. Her brief but blazing days of publicity made her name and face famous throughout the land and the heavy sentences lashed out on Bunker and the rest of his team must have seemed most proper in view of the enormity of their crime. I bathed in the public opinion, feeling the warmth of it although it was not directed at me, but behind the scenes I also came in for a fair bit of heat from another direction.

Stella took the whole business none too kindly. She had followed the case with close attention and it did not escape her that Terrence and Bernadette O'Mahoney were in some way acting as agents for the police. I insisted, particularly in Bernadette's case, that it was the right of a victim to speak out against those who assailed her – and being soft hearted, Stella had to go along to some extent with that view. But it still bothered her that I was linked up in some way with the O'Mahoneys. I'd brought them to the Albion Hotel and wished them on Stella, and here they were working with the police. Didn't that make me tainted with the same sort of association? I assured her it didn't, but she still went round for days, mumbling darkly to herself.

And how had I got myself mixed up with the O'Mahoneys in the first place? That was a question that caused me a great deal of soul-searching. I kept it nice and simple because that was the only way to play it. I knew nothing about their connection with the police. I'd found them in the street, thumbing a lift, and although I'd been unable to give them a lift (no car, you see, and I wasn't going to tell Stella about the Viva) I'd suggested they might go to the Albion for a night or two. They'd be all right there. I knew the lady who kept it. She was a generous soul, etc. etc.

And I suppose I can claim it did the trick. She seemed to swallow it at least half way down – and as time went on she stopped mumbling and grumbling about it. A couple of visits to her boudoir, a bacon buttie or two in her appetizing kitchen, all these things helped to push the matter from her mind.

In the circumstances, I had less trouble with Doreen. To be truthful, I'm sure she enjoyed the excitement of it. And even though she knew very well that I'd worked with Boggis on this occasion she didn't seem to cotton on that there was anything permanent about the arrangement. After all, Doreen herself had asked me to become involved in the Bernadette affair, otherwise I'd never have bothered with it at all.

Thank God, some of the same sort of thinking seemed to rub off on Bernadette. She and Doreen did a lot of private chatting and it was plain to me that, in Bernadette's eyes, it was Doreen who had brought me into the game. I was a useful thing to have around – a man-friend ready to help out when some emergency arose. Doreen had wanted to help Bernadette, she'd called me in on her side and I'd responded. Beyond that, I was innocent.

To this day I'm not sure what Terrence O'Mahoney thought. I hope he saw me in the same light as his missus saw me. But in any case it doesn't matter very much, because he eventually joined Bernadette in that place unknown, to live happily ever after as I said earlier. But before that happened he had one final function to attend – one more appearance before the majesty of the court – and this time he was on the receiving end.

He pleaded guilty to two charges. One of possessing firearms illegally – the other of driving a motor vehicle when unfit through drink. I was struck by the absolute dearth of detail placed before the court. I have a cutting still, from the local rag, which relates to the case and which is headed:

SUPERGRASS GIVEN LIGHT SENTENCE

The item names Terrence O'Mahoney and describes him as 'an arch criminal turned supergrass' but it has very little to say about the charges to which he pleaded guilty. He was sentenced to twelve months imprisonment – suspended for twelve months – and the judge made a pointed comment about leniency having been shown to O'Mahoney in view of the valuable assistance he had given to the police.

So far – so good, but the case left me with considerable doubts. I couldn't make head nor tail of the charges against him. It's easy to say, *what does it matter?* or *for God's sake leave it alone.* I've got the sort of curiosity that will never let go of a problem like that.

I had to be very patient though.

It was months later before I was able to corner Bert Boggis and squeeze the story out of him.

THIRTEEN

There is just one place in the entire district where Detective Sergeant Boggis and I can meet, sit together at a table and buy each other drinks. It's a club of sorts, but more than that I won't say. We don't go there very often, but if the occasion arises when we need to sit and chinwag for a long time, then we go. Such an occasion came at the end of the long string of court cases in which Boggis and his supergrass were involved.

"For want of a better term, he was the armourer," Boggis said. "And that of itself is a development I don't particularly want to see repeated. It will be repeated, I feel it in my bones, but if I can think of a way of trampling on future armourers till they get fed up of appointing them, that's what I aim to do."

"What the hell's an armourer?" I asked unhelpfully.

"Somebody who handles arms," he explained. "In O'Mahoney's case that includes everything, obtaining, storing, carrying, supplying, repairing, the lot. And in relation to shotguns it also included working on the damned things with a saw to produce those nasty little sawn-off things the modern robber likes to carry."

"Is that the way you cracked the first job?"

"Patience, Peeper. Give me time to tell it. The interesting thing about Terrence O'Mahoney is that he was specially imported from Ireland because of his skill with guns. Something happened in this town that I should have noticed, but I didn't notice it – not soon enough, anyway. The big lads got together. They made a policy decision that they were going to be using guns more often and that in everybody's interests – not the public interest of course, or the police interest, but everybody else's interest – they should have a man handy who could service guns. For each separate gang to have a gun expert would be an unnecessary duplication, so, like a society of horse dealers appointing a common blacksmith they clubbed together and employed O'Mahoney to look after their guns."

"Hell, I don't like the sound of that, Bert."

"Neither do I, and one of your permanent commissions from now on is to find out if they appoint a replacement for friend Terrence, when they do it and who the sod is. That way we'll be able to foreclose on him before he gets started. But let's go back to the man in question. He seems to have been a good one. He knew his stuff and he gave good service. In return he received a pretty good screw, which explains, amongst other things, why he could afford a house and a car. It was his car that let him down, you know."

"I didn't know – but I'm sure you're going to tell me."

"Well, it was the armed robbery at Hymie Crewe's place that sparked the whole thing off. We'd had quite a lot of nasty little jobs before that, as I'm sure you very well remember. But there were no leads coming in, and although I told you to go out and find out who was behind them all, as usual you turned up a big round damn all."

"That's not fair, Bert. I …"

"Fair be damned. You were sleeping on the job, Peeper. You weren't trying. Blast it, man, you were actually there at the time of the Crewe robbery – you stood there and watched it happen – but when I asked you about it I might as well have asked a roll of four-by-two. You knew all three of the men involved, but just because they had wool hats on you couldn't identify a single one of them – or so you told me. The truth was, you saw Swanky Alice and point blank refused to tell me. You could have cracked the job wide open and you refused. That's the sort of loyalty I get from you."

"I had a good reason, Bert. I had to think about ..."

"That's the trouble with you, Peeper, you do far too much thinking and not enough acting. If you got your finger out now and then we'd make a lot more progress. But as it happens, I didn't need help from you, because we helped ourselves in another way."

"You knocked Terrence off – that much is obvious."

"That's right. It was that same evening, right after the Crewe job. And it was the traffic branch that pulled him in. He was driving his car along the main drag at about fifty miles an hour in a thirty limit, so they pulled him in."

"Speeding, eh? That was Bunker's downfall. As a point of interest, Bert, did O'Mahoney have any clothes on?"

"Never mind Bunker, let me get on. After they'd stopped O'Mahoney they smelled his breath and it practically turned their tunic buttons green, never mind the breathalyser, but they shoved the bag in his hand and went through the motions and he finished up down at the station, giving samples of his blood."

"That's the bit that puzzles me, Bert. How the hell did you progress from a breathalyser job to a firearms charge?"

"Not difficult, Peeper. Just a matter of being careful

as you follow routine police procedure. What happened was that the traffic sergeant brought O'Mahoney's car to the nick, which is usual, and had a quick look through it, which is also usual. What wasn't very usual was what the sergeant found in the boot – two sawn-off shotguns and a Luger. He had enough sense to leave them alone and send for me."

"So Terrence O'Mahoney was involved in the robbery?"

"Was he hell, you silly piecan. Not directly, anyway. As I said in the beginning, he was the armourer. It was his job to deliver the guns prior to the job and collect them from a prearranged place when the job was over. He'd been out to pick them up, but on the way he'd taken a few jars too many – hence the big discovery."

"So it was O'Mahoney who shopped the others."

"All in good time it was, but not straight away by any means. It may interest you to know, old chum, that when I took you to the nick as witness, O'Mahoney was already in there, being spoken to by the traffic lads. I'd no sooner kicked you out than they were after me to tell me about the guns they'd found. I went to see O'Mahoney and he wouldn't tell me the size of his bloody shoes."

"So you worked on him and made him talk. The old police brutality bit. I know you, Boggis. You beat the poor bugger till he had to confess. You tortured him until he talked."

"He didn't have to talk, Peeper. In fact, it was well into the following day before he started talking."

"You're joking. You had Swanky Alice and his mates in that same night. It was in the papers next morning."

"My my, you have done your homework. And as it happens you've worked it out all wrong, which is typical of you. Sure we knocked Proud off, and Nelson

and Field, but not because of anything Terrence
O'Mahoney told us. They were a bit shaken, I can tell
you. They didn't know who the hell had shopped them.
They thought it was you."

"And don't I know it. That was your bloody fault as
well."

"I deny it. The point is, Peeper, nobody shopped
them. All we did was turn our scenes-of-crime lads loose
on the guns. There was nothing at all on the Luger, but
the sawn-offs, hell, it was corn in Egypt. We got a full set
of Proud's dabs off one and a full set of Bent Nelson's
off the other. They were so good that we didn't wait till
morning. We drove straight to headquarters, checked
the files and knocked all three of them off on the way
home."

"All three of them? But I thought …"

"And you're quite right, Peeper. We didn't have
enough on John Field, but we were looking for three
men, and when we found Proud and Nelson, Field was
with them, so he got arrested under the
chance-your-arm rules of the common law. Oddly
enough, picking him up was enough to break him. I
don't mean really break him, Peeper. A man like Field
never confesses. But he said enough to convince us that
we had the right man, told a few lies that we could
disprove and then capped it all by having a cartridge
case in his pocket that he'd taken out of the Luger. I've
got to tell you a little bit more about Field, Peeper, and
you might not like it."

"Try me."

"He gave me your name. He was sneering like mad
and he accused me of having paid you to shop him. I
asked him to explain that, and he wouldn't, but we
know why, don't we. He couldn't tell me that you'd
seen the job happen, except by admitting *he* was

there."

"And you rushed out to warn me. Thanks very much, Bert. Come to think of it, you had another chance to warn me, next day, when I came to see you. But did you warn me? Did you bloody hell. You turned me out like a sacrificial lamb."

"That was entirely unforeseen, Peeper. Anyway, it's water under the bridge. The point is, you hadn't told me about Proud and company, so how could I anticipate they might go for you?"

"I anticipated it, Bert. I told you it was certain to happen. And what did you do – you laughed in my face."

"Now you're not being fair. If you cast your mind back, Peeper, you'll remember it was me who saved you from Parrott and his mates."

"You were a bit late arriving, Bert. I'd had my drubbing by the time the cops showed up. But I'll admit this much, they did me a real favour, coming when they did. But that struck me as a very stage-managed affair. How the hell did you know where to go? How the hell did you know they were holding me?"

"We didn't, Peeper – and that's the truth of it. When the inspector rang me and said you were with Parrott's lot it took me completely by surprise. He wanted to lock you up. I had to go and intercede with the superintendent in order to get you off the hook. No, don't bother thanking me. It's not gratitude I'm after, Peeper, it's just a bit of understanding."

I didn't give a damn what he was after. What he was going to get, if he didn't buck up, was a hefty kick on the shin, accompanied by a lot of swear words.

"You're dodging the issue, Bert," I told him. "What I asked you is how the hell did you happen to latch on to the Parrott gang?"

"Ah now, that's a longish story. It's tied up with our friend O'Mahoney again. That was a busy night for me, what with Swanky Alice and his mates being locked up, but I still found time to talk to Terrence – and he nearly gave himself a tonsillectomy through talking about how nothing would make him talk. I'm being straight about that, Peeper. When I was talking to you, the following day, and you were telling me how you'd lost your backbone and were running scared about a few local thugs not being pleased with you, at that stage O'Mahoney hadn't said a word that was in any way useful to me."

"But he started to talk – is that it?"

"And how. It came on all of a sudden, like a duckling learning to swim. One minute he was granite, the next, putty."

"That's interesting. What do you suppose changed him?"

"I think I know what changed him, Peeper. It didn't all come out at the time, but later on, after I'd got to know Terrence rather better, he told me a lot of little things that I was able to add up. Looking back on our acquaintanceship I believe I know very well why he started to talk, but I didn't know it at the time."

"All right then. If you know, tell me."

"O.K. The start point was when Terrence found out about Swanky Alice and Bent Nelson and John Field. Not when they were arrested, but later, when Terrence learned *how* they'd been arrested and *why*. He got those answers from me, of course. I was using the story to try to get him to confess, and it didn't seem to have any effect on him at all. But in fact it had affected him greatly. He began to imagine that he'd be blamed – by the gangs, that is – for the arrest of the three robbers. It was his fault, you see. He'd allowed the evidence to fall into the hands of the police and as a result his mates were in the cells. So he mooned about it – and he started to wonder if he'd be out of a job when this was over – if they'd sack him."

"Sack him! They'd more than likely croak him."

"He must have considered that, too. But the point is, Peeper, the guilt complex stayed with him for a while – until he started looking for reasons to justify himself, and that was really when the rot set in. It wasn't his fault at all. The real fault lay with a man called Peter David Parrott."

"So he sent you out to find Parrott?"

"Easy now. Take your time. What had really happened, it seems, was that Parrott had organised the robbery at Crewe's place. He'd organised all the robberies in fact. Digressing for a minute, Peter David Parrott is well known in the midlands as a top operator and he came to this town last year, when Frenchy Watts and Stevie Brooks went the way of all bad men. Parrott was fast becoming the king-pin of all crime operations. It was Parrott who arranged to employ Terrence O'Mahoney in the first place. Parrott had the knack of drawing men together. He was starting to use members of gangs that had once been run quite separately to act together and carry out bigger raids. He was a bastard, was Parrott, and I'm bloody relieved he only had a very short reign.

"But coming back to O'Mahoney, he'd been given the task of laying the guns on for the Crewe job. He had to supply them shortly before the raid, then hang about in the vicinity in his car, with the boot open, so that the robbers could drop the guns in there and be rid of them. Notice, he didn't stay close to the betting shop and he wasn't the getaway car. The getaway car was driven by Lenny Bethel, and his job was to drive to a certain quiet street, stop momentarily while the robbers dropped their guns into O'Mahoney's car, then drive off like the clappers. That way, if the getaway car was stopped – no guns. And if the gun car was stopped – no robbers. It wasn't a bad scheme, Peeper, nor all that original. But the point is, it worked – till Terrence decided to shoot his mouth off.

"Well, the first mistake happened at that stage. John Field stuck to the rules – he wiped his Luger clean. Not that a Luger ever carries much in the way of prints unless you're very lucky, but Field was taking no chances. The other two – well, you know Bent Nelson and Swanky Alice, they're thick as pig shit. They knew they should have wiped their sawn-offs, but they were much too chuffed with the success of the mission to worry about minor details like that."

"You said he blamed Parrott. Why didn't he blame those two dozy sods? I can't see that it was Parrott's fault."

"Once again you interrupt – and you do it badly. The point is, O'Mahoney thought nothing at that stage. It was only much later, when he'd considered all the other factors, that he noticed the first fundamental error, and by that time he was firmly set against Parrott. Because Parrott was responsible for O'Mahoney's condition."

"What condition?"

"His drunkenness. No, more than his drunkenness, his laxity."

"You've lost me a bit, Bert."

"Then let me bring you back to the straight and narrow. As armourer, Terrence O'Mahoney was a very conscientious man. His job, having collected the guns, was to get them away as quickly as possible and stash them with the rest of the weapons. The rest of the weapons? Oh yes, they had quite a considerable stock, Peeper, all kept in a strong room at the back of a warehouse that belongs to the syndicate. I'm glad to say we collected all that stuff – and some pretty way-out armaments there are, too – but that's nothing to do with this story, so we'll press on. Left to his own devices, O'Mahoney would have been rid of those guns within half an hour, but he ran into Parrott, and Parrott delayed him.

"To me, that's still a bit of a puzzler, but O'Mahoney swears it's true. Here we have Peter David Parrott, a stickler for the rules and an iron man when it came to imposing group discipline. Yet he met his armourer, took him to a pub and plied him with drink *before he'd had time to get rid of the guns*. You could understand it if Parrott hadn't realised the position, but it seems he knew the position very well. O'Mahoney told him about the guns, refused drinks, pleaded with Parrott to let him go and finish his job. But Parrott was in merry mood. He was feeling his strength a bit, I think, convincing himself that he now ran the town and nothing could get in his way. So he kept pouring whisky down O'Mahoney's throat, and O'Mahoney's resistance was entirely overcome.

"Well, you know the outcome of that boozing session, and maybe you're a bit nearer to understanding why O'Mahoney began to blame Parrott. But you're only half way, yet, to understanding why O'Mahoney finally decided to go the whole way."

"I'm ahead of you, Bert. He was afraid of Parrott."

"Balderdash, but exactly the sort of thing you'd think of not being one of nature's heroes. No, O'Mahoney was afraid of nobody. On the other hand, he did have a fear. It was a fear of prison. Not the ordinary fear of prison that we all feel, but a fear associated with his wife, Bernadette. Bernadette was pregnant – and O'Mahoney was looking forward to being a father. He didn't want to spend the years of his child's youth wrapped round with concrete and iron bars. And the reason why that fear obsessed him was because he knew Parrott was the root cause. But for Parrott, he'd be in the clear, but because Parrott had virtually forced him to break the rules he was facing a long time inside – not just for drunk driving, which would have brought him a fine, but for offences concerning firearms.

"In the end, Peeper, as you'll know if you read the papers, we put only a token minimum of charges against O'Mahoney. That was done with full official approval. But at the earlier stage, when he was in the cells brooding about Parrott, he had time to let his imagination run riot about all the charges we were likely to throw at him. As an accomplice, he was tied up with nearly all the crime that had happened over the past year. Well, with his mind in that state he had neither fear of nor love for Peter David Parrott, and as the hours went by *he talked himself into grassing*. You will have your little joke, Peeper, about police brutality and all that, but none was used on O'Mahoney and none necessary. He sent for me. He didn't ask for any favours – he just said, in effect, *pin your ears back and listen*.

"He didn't just talk about Parrott. As you'll realise, he started to talk about all sorts of people who were tied up in all sorts of things. People like O'Mahoney are funny that way. They're like a river blocked off by a dam. They lie dormant till they find a hole in the dam, then they begin to trickle through, which enlarges the hole, which increases the flow – and so on. In the later stages he began to grow pleased with himself. He felt the power his knowledge gave him over other men. He *wanted* to shop people, wanted to see them locked up, wanted to know he was the oracle guiding me and my men to thieves and rogues by the van-load. We really had him going well, Peeper. And then, as you know, the buggers nipped in and took Bernadette and after that, he …"

"Never mind after that, Bert. What about before that? So he told you about Parrott – but he didn't tell you where to go, or when, or that Parrott was having a heart to heart talk with me."

"There was an element of chance in that. I'm pleased to say it was me who kicked it off. After you'd left me that day, I went into town for a stroll. O'Mahoney wasn't talking at that stage. I saw three men in a black Rover car – Lenny Bethel, Chester Moreland and Big Ginger Fish. I just said to myself, *on your way you bloody heathen swine*, and thought no more about it. Then I went back to the nick, just in time to be summoned to O'Mahoney's cell and witness the first breach of the dam.

"He started naming names and linking names with crimes. He even supplied a lot of details I knew I could prove. Effectively, he was more than tipping me off, he was proving my cases for me. I had a clerk in, scribbling down a long list of names, and quite early on he mentioned Bethel, Moreland and Fish. I didn't leave him, but I took a minute to tell Control Room that I'd seen these three in town, a short while before, in a black Rover. I asked them to chuck the details out to all patrols.

"The next report came pretty quickly. The Rover had been seen heading out towards Sephton Park

Estate, only this time there was an extra body on board. I never dreamed it was you, Peeper, but I did wonder who it might be. So I popped the question to Terrence."

"That'll be Parrott," he told me. "He's living in a big house out that way. Took it over from a fella called Watts."

"So you know the rest of it, Peeper. I moved a bit rapid, swore out some warrants and passed 'em out to the traffic lads for execution. There was no warrant for you because I didn't know you were there. No, let me rephrase that. I had no reason to issue a warrant for you."

"Thank's Bert. I'm pleased to hear it. I was pleased to hear it at the time, I remember. I have a nasty little feeling that if the cops hadn't shown up I wouldn't be here now. But then, within a few hours, the heat suddenly went off me. Why was that?"

"That happened because Terrence O'Mahoney proved to be an awkward little bastard – just like you are most of the time. I wanted to play it quietly – hell, that's the only way you *can* play a thing like this – but Terrence was proud of himself. He'd psyched himself up to spill every bean in the can and he wanted the world to know about it. So we had a battle down there at the nick. I kept trying to keep him out of sight and he kept snatching conversations with every solicitor who came in the place, every prisoner, every visitor. It was quite hopeless. Within a very short time, the truth was out about who was responsible for grassing, and evidently that's when they stopped blaming you."

"He must have been mad, Bert. Did it ever occur to him that they'd strike back? All he had in the world was his family. It's easy to be wise after things have happened, but in O'Mahoney's situation it's a wonder he didn't *anticipate* that they'd snatch his missus."

"You're right for once, Peeper, and he didn't. The man was so bloody cocksure, he never gave a thought to reprisals. I carry a certain amount of guilt myself. *I* should have anticipated a move like that, never mind Terrence. The reason I didn't is because I was too slow to realise the word was out. I kept clinging to the hope that O'Mahoney was still my secret – I even said as much to you, at a very late stage – and by the time I admitted I was wrong, they'd nipped in and snatched the woman."

"And that took the wind out of O'Mahoney's sails."

"Funnily enough, Peeper, it didn't. I find it hard to describe O'Mahoney's mood when he heard that Bernadette was missing, but I'll do my best. He was furious, naturally, and he was afraid for them (by which I mean Bernadette and her unborn child) but far from making him repent his ways, the incident made him stronger. The only concession he would make, at that stage, was that he refused to back up some of the stuff he'd given me – that explains why I had to let a lot of people go – but even then he was promising me that I'd have them all in the end. He played a game – a very serious game, but a game nonetheless. He made it appear that he was accepting their bargain by withholding testimony, but to me he was saying something quite different. He was saying, *look – for Christ's sake find her and get her back safely. If you save her, I'll give you more information about the crooks in this area than you ever dreamed possible. If you fail, if they kill her, then I'll see the bastards in hell, and all their muckers along with them. Either way, you'll get the dope, but I want it the first way. I want her safe. And until you find her, one way or the other, I'm shutting my trap.* He thinks a hell of a lot of his wife and kid, Peeper. And he's very grateful to you, by the way.

He asked me to pass on his thanks."

"Very nice of him."

"And so did his wife. Bernadette was very pleased with you too. Hell, I'm pleased with you myself. You're a likeable rogue."

"Never mind that. Tell me about his house. He was very, very displeased that day you rang him at the Albion. So would I be, if my house was burned down, but it seemed to be more than that. He obviously thought it had been done on purpose, by his enemies."

"And so it had, Peeper. By Bunker Hunker, out of sheer spite, because you'd pulled the rug from under him. I can say that – and it's true – but I can't prove it. Believe me, I've put a lot of time in trying to sort that job out. The elements of arson are all there – paraffin, the match stalks, the piling up of fuel, the various different seats of fire – but I can't get enough to pin it on Bunker, even though I have some evidence to show he was in the district at the time. So that will have to stay in the list of undetected crime, Peeper. It doesn't bother me a great deal. Bunker will be inside for many years to come, which is just punishment, and with all the crime we've cleared up lately, we can stand a few that are uncleared. In fact, it's quite possible that Bunker helped me in a curious way by having a go at O'Mahoney's property. It made O'Mahoney very mad indeed. He'd already told me a lot, but I think the fire drove him on to even greater efforts." He paused and gave me an old-fashioned look. "He was a very useful man, our Terrence. Does it occur to you, Peeper, that in a few short days he cleared more crime for me than you've ever done in all your rotten little puff?"

"Thank's very much. You're saying I've been superseded?"

"Nothing of the sort. You're still my never failing

seam of ore. O'Mahoney was a flash in the pan – a bloody big flash, it's true – but once a flash is over, it's over. And he was paid well for his pains. He'll never want again. But it follows that I can never use him again, because he'll never be in a position to find things out. You on the other hand …"

"Speaking of being well paid, Bert, what about me? When do I collect? How much have I got coming?"

He gave me a look that boded ill.

"You, you greedy little sod. Why should anybody pay you? You never did anything to clear these crimes up. My informant was O'Mahoney. He gave me everything I needed."

"Not everything. He didn't find Bernadette. He didn't put you wise to Bunker's house and the set-up there. He didn't warn you when the clouds were gathering. He didn't organise the little deception that got you out of the shit. Think about it, Bert. Without me, the whole project could easily have come adrift."

"Without Doreen, you mean. It was Doreen who took the risks that day. She was the one who took *all* the risks. That mob might have torn her limb from limb, but she faced it, and won through. I'm surprised at you, Peeper. You're such a mercenary little sod. You want paying for everything – including the work Doreen did. Well you won't get it. You won't swing that on me."

It didn't surprise me, of course. Getting money out of Bert Boggis had always been akin to quenching your thirst with sawdust. I knew he was laying it on thick. I knew there'd be something to come in the end, because he simply daren't *not* pay me. But he wanted me to haggle and bargain. He wanted me to struggle to make out a case, so that he could give in with a great show of reluctance. Well, I was all through haggling. I gave him a glare that was calculated to singe his eye-brows and I snapped:

"Very well, then. Pay Doreen."

And he did.